TO GAIN FOREVER

A GAINING LOVE NOVELLA

TANYA EAVENSON

"*To Gain a Mommy*, by Tanya Eavenson is a sweet novella-length Christian romance. The plot is straight-forward and plausible. The characters are well-developed, and Ms. Eavenson's writing style is smooth and enjoyable. For those who like romance with strong Christian underpinnings, this is a good pick!" ~Carolyn

"*To Gain a Mommy* is story of former sweethearts with a mountain of hurt between them. Helping them through their journey to try to get past the pain are two adorable children, a loveable dog, and a mom/grandmother who knows the importance of dealing with hurts now. Add in a beach setting, and, oh, did I mention chocolate? If you're a fan of watching God heal hearts and bring sweet forgiveness, you definitely don't want to miss this one. And I dare say, you'll love the rest of the series as well. Buy. This. Book! You'll be glad you did!" ~Marie

"I love reading everything by this author! She brings her stories to life and holds your attention. This story is sweet, romantic, heartfelt, uplifting, and challenging. The couple embark on a journey of healing, seeking God, and allowing Him to work in their lives. It's a great read. I highly recommend this book!" ~Kris

"An enjoyable novella with great multifaceted characters that are realistic and with whom the reader can empathize and fall in love with. A plot that is interesting, engaging, enjoyable and a great easy read. For a novella, the author was able to develop a full story that isn't lacking in any one area, has dropped underlying issue and minor storylines." ~AJK

"It was so nice to see that Patrick Reynolds gets his happily ever after. I felt so sorry for him in the book *To Gain a Mommy*. This story made me realize that God has plans for each of us and we just need to be open to them. If you are a pet owner or love pets you will laugh at how inept Patrick is with animals. Thank goodness he is not that way with children since he is a pediatrician. I also liked the second chance theme in this story which made the story even better. What a fun, heartfelt story of finding love when you might least expect to." ~Lori

"This is the first of Tanya's books that I have read. I will definitely be purchasing and reading more books by her. She has entwined a thriller with love & Christianity. It is definitely a great read! I highly recommend it." ~Charlotte

"Brice and Madi are likable, well-rounded characters working together in a dangerous situation. The suspense kept me turning pages as I became more invested in their safety and in their growing attraction for each other. I also enjoyed the brief glimpses of characters from the first two novellas in the series. I've enjoyed all three novellas in this series and look forward to reading more books by Tanya Eavenson." ~E.M.

"I loved this book! It was a great romance watching the relationship strengthen between the two characters and suspenseful as I did not know what would happen to her or if there would be danger! Great book and loved to read similar." ~Jay

To Gain Forever

Published by All Roads Publishing

Copyright © 2020 by Tanya Eavenson

On file at the Library of Congress in Washington, DC.

ISBN 978-1-945981-06-7

Scripture quotations, whether quoted or paraphrased by the characters, are taken from the King James Version of the Bible.

Cover Design by Suzanne D. Williams, Graphic Design

ry not to stare.

Karianne Beckett nodded in the direction of the leashed cat leading its owner across the street. "There's the guy I was telling you about."

"Where am I looking?" Melissa asked a little too loudly from beside her on the wooden bench.

"Shhh. Next to my car," she whispered.

The cat and its owner strolled outside the perimeter of the fence. Of course, the man certainly wouldn't dare come inside. Who in their right mind would bring a cat to a dog park?

Based on how all the dogs around her had traded playing for barking, she wasn't the only one who noticed their arrival. Her sweet boy was among them. "Jake," she called.

He looked her way, tongue lolling, then trotted over.

"Good boy." The *good* spoken an octave higher replicated his training. She smiled at her Lab, once again thankful for his retirement from service in Iraq and

1

Afghanistan. She wouldn't know what to do without her companion. Whoever said dogs were man's best friend didn't know they could be a woman's too.

Melissa elbowed her. "You weren't kidding. He's handsome."

She grinned. "Are we talking about Jake or the cat walker?"

Her friend chuckled.

"He's not bad either." Karianne's gaze followed him as he and the cat topped the hill and disappeared behind the trees.

"I'd say he's about mid-thirties like you. How long has he been coming here?"

"Not sure. I first saw him last week. Since then, he's been here most days I have."

"So in a week's time you've not made contact?"

Did his nearly running her and Jake over two days ago count? Nah. And Melissa didn't need to know of their encounter, or how the man apologized profusely through his car window. His soft brown eyes had sunk into hers, but it was the concern in his tone that touched something deep within her that she didn't want to feel.

She hadn't seen him since.

"He has a cat. I think Jake might have a problem with that."

Melissa rose from the bench and snatched up her keys. "Just give Jake a treat. He always listens to you. Besides, there's a huge difference between a cat and IED caches."

Karianne still couldn't imagine Jake on the battlefield, or imagine all that he'd experienced as a bomb dog. His life was different now and so was hers. The past was the past, and she was leaving it there.

"I gotta get back to the hospital. Call me tonight. We still need to talk about your plans for the balloon race and festival. Brian's family is coming."

"When you say family, does that include his brother, Harper?"

With a sly little smile, Melissa shrugged and turned toward the gate. "Bye." She waved over her shoulder.

Karianne shook her head. She couldn't fault her friend. Melissa's brother-in-law, Harper, was nice. Okay, more than nice, but was she ready to get back into the dating mix? It had been three years. And Harper's visit last year didn't count. Or did it? They'd spent time talking about life and their mutual interest in dogs, and they'd had lunch together during Helen, Georgia's, balloon festival.

Still, she wasn't sure she'd ever be ready for anything deeper.

With a sigh, she called Jake, who'd wandered off to play with the other dogs. He came willingly, tail wagging. She rubbed behind his ears and stoked his yellow coat. "Ready to go, buddy? I've gotta get to the chapel. There's a wedding tomorrow night, and I still have tons to do." She stood and collected her water.

At her Jeep, Karianne let Jake in the back and circled around to the driver's side.

And came face-to-face with the handsome cat walker.

～

3

Trey had almost dragged Whiskers down the hill behind him in his need to reach the auburn-haired woman before she left. He'd seen her for the first time last week during one of his dog park visits. He'd been strolling in the open field outside the fenced-in area when a chuckle caught his attention. He hadn't known anyone was there, but when he turned and saw the way her nose wrinkled and her hazel eyes watched in disbelief as Whiskers glided along the grass, she'd drawn a smile from him, and a closer look.

Granted, he deserved the jaw drop she gave him as he passed. Who took their cat for a walk to a dog park? But the place he was staying was across the street. When Dillon mentioned a vacancy at his townhome during the time of the balloon festival and his business with Helen's city council, he'd jumped at the opportunity.

Today, the impeccable timing compelled him to jog through the same open field where he'd first seen her and into a parking lot where she was putting her dog in a Jeep.

They met near the driver's side door and he stopped, unsure of what to say. "Hi," he blurted, breathless from the short run.

The woman stopped, and her lips pulled into a tight frown as she met his gaze. "I didn't see you standing there."

Of course she hadn't. "I was heading across the street." *But wanted to see you first.* "Didn't mean to scare you. It seems I have a habit of doing that. I'm sorry about the other day on the hill—again."

She looked in that direction for a split second, then

refocused on him. "I take it you're new in town. I haven't seen you until recently."

Man, what color were her eyes? He'd thought hazel, but... "I am. Here on business. And you?"

"Lived here most of my life."

"I'm Trey Scott." His cat nudged his legs as she wound between them. "This beggar-of-attention is Whiskers."

She smiled down at the cat. "Hi, Whiskers. I'm sure my fur-buddy would like to meet you too. He's the beast drooling on the window behind me. His name is Jake."

Trey chuckled. That was exactly what the dog was doing.

She extended her hand to him. "And I'm Karianne."

He grasped her hand. Small. Soft. *No last name?* "Unusual name. I like it."

"Jake is a pretty common one."

"I meant yours."

She slipped her fingers from his. "I know." A light flush tinged her cheeks. "Thanks. Where are you from? You have a slight accent. I can't place it."

She was an inquisitive one. "Ohio."

"Really? Which part?"

He caught the inflection of the question. "Mansfield. Have you been to Ohio before?"

She paused for a moment. He wasn't sure she'd heard him until she shook her head.

"No, but we have a lot of tourists that come through. They either celebrate the holidays, attend one of our annual festivals, or marry here. You'd be surprised how many people I've met." She glanced at the Jeep. "I should go. I've got to get Jake home. It was nice meeting you."

"Same here." And with that, he swooped down and lifted Whiskers in his arms.

As she left the parking lot, Trey crossed the street to the townhouse, all the while thinking about Karianne. He unlocked the front door and set Whiskers in the foyer. She moseyed into the living room as if she owned the place. But this wasn't her home, or his.

Three weeks. That's all the time they had in Helen before heading back to Ohio.

"Lord, you know I don't believe in falling for someone at first sight."

But was she the one?

CHAPTER 2

*H*olding a bouquet of fresh peonies and dusty-pink roses, Karianne focused on her steps. The day she had received a call from the bride and groom, she'd known this would be hard, but nothing had prepared her for the deluge of memories that washed over her as she walked down the aisle. The same aisle she'd never had the privilege to walk.

"Betsy." Her voice cracked, and she swallowed.

Her assistant looked up from the clipboard she held.

"I've tied a string within the bouquet to keep the baby's breath from slipping and taking the rest of the flowers with it."

"You always know how to fix things."

Karianne forced a smile, then headed back up the aisle toward the double doors of the chapel. She couldn't fix everything.

Not her broken heart.

Not her dying fiancé.

Would she ever meet a man she could trust? Did one even exist?

Karianne paused in the foyer, out of view of everyone. She had to get a grip. She was the chapel's wedding planner, and the bride was due any moment. "Pull it together, girl. You knew eventually someone would plan a wedding on this day."

Within the same breath, the double doors opened, and there stood the bride in the entrance, clothed in a beautiful scooped-neck ball gown. Her mother was the first to enter.

It's showtime. "Mrs. Stevens, Brittney, don't you both look lovely." She took the bride by the hand. "Your dress is perfect. Tom won't know what hit him."

"That's my hope." The bride fanned herself.

"Then let's get you to your room before the groom's party arrives. The room is chilled to your liking."

Something was nagging Trey, but he couldn't put his finger on it. He ran through the events of his day, and nothing seemed out of the ordinary, except for his meeting with the city council.

And what a meeting it was. If everything went according to plan, his bid for the city's annual fireworks show at the end of the balloon festival would soon be granted. The city had asked for a sample of his work, and soon he'd give everyone a show they wouldn't forget.

Trey went to the garage and gathered precut fiber-glass mortar tubes, wooden planks, and other materials that housed the fireworks, and set them in separate piles. With his adrenaline high and sleep nowhere in sight, he might as well start constructing the vertical rack.

Settled on the floor, he squared several wooden planks and reached for his cordless drill. The nagging feeling struck him harder than before and settled in his chest.

At a loss, he glanced around at Dillon's neatly stacked shelves, tools, and cabinets, and murmured a prayer. "Lord, thank you for the opportunity with the city. Thank you for blessing and growing the business. But this uneasiness I'm feeling… What is it, Lord? Is there something I should have done? Something I should be doing?"

Maybe he should bring his car in the garage. For added workspace, he'd parked in the driveway. It would be a tight fit, but he'd manage.

Trey nabbed his keys from the kitchen counter and pressed the garage remote as he left the mud room. With a hum, the door lifted, and darkness seeped in where he stood. A light rose from across the street and grew brighter once he reached his car. "Who would be at the dog park after hours?"

Curious, he went back in for his phone, locked the main house, and left through the garage. As he crossed the street, a dog barked.

What were the chances it was Karianne's dog or that the woman who held his thoughts captive would be here now? Turning on his phone's flashlight, Trey pointed it in the direction he heard the barking. The beam skimmed across a familiar figure chasing something. "Karianne?" He continued walking toward the gate.

"Guilty as charged."

Maybe it was the dark and being unable to see her clearly, but she sounded … different. Fragile, almost. "Are you alone?"

"Jake's with me."

He searched the fenced area, still unable to see her. "Everything all right?"

"It's locked. I'm outside the park. At the second bench."

He pointed the light at the grass and followed a worn path in the ground to where she sat with a tennis ball in her right hand. Jake lay at her feet, tail wagging. She wore jeans and an oversize shirt, but otherwise she looked like she'd just came from a date. Her hair was up, make-up was on, and a bracelet on her left wrist sparkled like diamonds in the flashlight's beam. She shouldn't be out here alone, even with Jake. "Do you come here often at night?"

"Jake needed to get out." She shrugged. "He'd been cooped up all day."

Was that all? By the way she avoided his gaze, he wasn't sure. He turned off the light. "Do you mind if I join you?"

"I have to warn you, I'm not good company right now."

"That's all right. I am."

She looked at him then, and he was thankful his eyes had adjusted to the darkness, because the smile she gave him made his heart pump faster. He lowered to the bench next to her, and the gentle scent of vanilla reached him.

"So tell me about yourself, Trey Scott. I don't share a bench with just anyone. You could be a mass killer for all

I know." Karianne threw the tennis ball, and Jake scurried after it.

"That I'm not, and I have a feeling you don't think so, or you wouldn't have invited me to sit with you."

"True. The man's house you're staying in, Dillon, he's a good friend, and I know for certain he only allows family or close personal friends to use his place. If he trusts you, then I can share my bench."

"Yeah, he's a great guy."

Jake brought Karianne the tennis ball, and she tossed it again. "How do you know Dillon?"

"We grew up together. Went to the same schools. Roommates at Ohio State."

"Huh. But he graduated from Georgia Institute of Technology."

"He transferred, and his parents moved with him."

"So you're both engineers?"

"Yeah, Dillon is a chemical engineer. I'm a civil engineer. I started out going for the same degree as Dillon, but my family pushed me toward being a civil engineer. My brother and I have the same degree. It's good for business."

Jake ran toward them, but this time Trey held out his hand for the ball. Instead of Jake handing him the tennis ball as he'd done for Karianne, he dropped it to the ground and feverishly began sniffing Trey's hand.

Karianne tried to get Jake's attention but it was useless. "Jake. Heel."

Jake immediately sat between them, and if Trey didn't know better, the dog was looking him straight in the eye. "I'm not sure he knows what to think of me."

"I don't know what came over him. You must have something on your hand he likes."

"I guess so."

She looked to Jake and spoke the words Jake's handler had instructed her to say. "Freedom. Life." Immediately, Jake went for the tennis ball on the ground and dropped it into Karianne's hand. She threw it. "So, a family business?"

It took him a moment to get his thoughts together. "My brother and I own the family construction company. When our dad retired, he left us the business."

"Was it an easy transition?"

"Dad's had me training for the job since I could walk. It was easy for me, but if you ask Dad, I'm not sure what he'd say. Mom keeps giving him honey-do lists. I think he's working more now that he's retired." He chuckled.

"It must be nice working with your family."

"It is, but it leaves little room for branching out on your own."

"What do you mean?"

"The normal story. Family business is important. You don't want to let anyone down. Dreams are put on hold. I thought being the youngest would make a difference, that my brother would take over and I'd help out from time to time, but we're in it fifty-fifty."

He looked to her. What did she think about that? He didn't want to seem ungrateful. He loved his family and enjoyed the business, but it wasn't his dream. He wanted more, a successful business he built from the ground up, a wife that loved him enough to encourage his dreams, and a family of his own.

He hadn't told anyone but his brother and Dillon about his small fireworks company, and guilt over it had been eating at him for months. This trip to Helen was the jumpstart his future needed. A future so close he could almost feel it.

Karianne stood as Jake ran toward her. "I think we're going to go. He's had enough exercise for tonight, and I haven't eaten."

"Does that mean the interrogation is over?"

The corner of her mouth lifted. "You're right. You were good company. Thanks." She looked to the dog. "Come, Jake."

Trey stood and quickly followed. "To be fair, I think I should have the same opportunity to ask you twenty questions."

At the Jeep she unlocked the vehicle, and Jake jogged to the door. "Was it twenty? To be *fair*, I'd say about ten."

"Then ten it is."

She let Jake in the backseat and closed the door. "I have another wedding in two days. I should be here about the same time."

"You're a wedding planner?"

"I am. Now that leaves you with nine questions to go."

"Then I better stop while I'm ahead." He opened the driver's side door and held it for her. "Until Thursday, then."

She slid in. The vehicle's overhead light shone down on her lovely smile. "Night."

He closed the door and gave her a small nod before

she backed out of the park and headed toward Main Street. Her rear lights faded into the night.

Would Karianne really be interested in dating a man who made fireworks for a living instead of choosing to be a successful contractor? One who lived 755 miles away?

"Lord, was that what the uneasiness was all about? I needed to see her tonight?" Whatever the case, the turmoil was gone.

He realized then that when he asked if she was all right, she never answered.

CHAPTER 3

*K*arianne sought her best friend through the cafeteria windows, hoping to catch sight of her in the hospital's corridors before she entered. They hadn't talked last night as planned, but they did text to confirm their lunch. It was twenty-three minutes past two, and Melissa was still a no-show.

From her chair near the checkout counter, Karianne couldn't help overhearing the hospital staffers at the next table murmuring about protocol. She checked her messages again, trying not to eavesdrop on their conversation. Nothing. Perhaps her friend was in the middle of something important and couldn't text.

She eyed the cheesecake she'd spotted when she first entered the cafeteria, and her stomach growled. Since early this morning, she'd been busy with wedding preparations and hadn't had time to eat. If she didn't now, another opportunity wouldn't come until after Jake went to the park.

She glanced around and narrowed in on a gowned

patient being wheeled past the window. Wasn't that the same man she'd seen before? Melissa had once mentioned that wheelchair patients were prohibited in this area, but today she'd seen several, some crossing her path more than once, like this man. Curiosity winning out, she tuned back into the conversation one table over.

"What's happened? Have you heard anything?" someone said.

"Something is going on and no one is talking." Another voice lifted above the hum of cafeteria chatter.

"I heard there's an investigation."

She turned an ear in their direction.

"What type of investigation?"

"Not sure, but someone mentioned the FBI."

Karianne's body went stiff. *FBI? What on earth is going on?* A chill ran up her spine. *Where was Melissa?* She grabbed her cell from the table and texted her.

R U OK?

One of the staffers stood. "Hey, we gotta go." A moment later, they were dumping their trash in the bins near the door.

She glanced their direction in time to catch their profiles as they disappeared into the hospital's corridor. Burgundy scrubs. The color of their scrubs represented their department, so she'd have to ask Melissa what department wore burgundy—if she ever returned her messages.

A text came through. *Melissa is driving. —Sent from my car.*

Driving?

Karianne's phone rang, and she checked the screen. Melissa. She answered quickly. "What's going on?"

"I'm fine. A patient was transported to another hospital but didn't have the paperwork. I know we're supposed to have lunch, but ..." She sighed. "It's been a crazy day, and it's only going to get worse."

"Paperwork? You drove to another hospital to give actual paperwork?"

"Our computers are down."

"Hey, I overheard some things in the cafeteria while I was waiting." She pushed from her chair, grabbed her purse, and headed out of the hospital. She passed a man and woman uniformed in navy blue and turned back to see the bold yellow insignia. "Something about FBI," she muttered.

"I heard the same."

"Want to tell me what's going on?"

"This is bad, Karianne. There was a security breach, and our system was hijacked. We have limited access to the computer systems, and we're having to turn new patients away. We're continuing to care for the patients in the hospital." She sighed again. "But who knows how this will affect people's lives."

"I can't believe it. Do they know who's behind it?"

"Not sure. If they do, they aren't saying. I'm heading back to the hospital now. I can't imagine what today will hold. I'll call you to reschedule lunch."

"Not to worry." At her car, she opened the door and slid into the driver's seat. "Besides, I know you wanted to talk about Harper."

"And about our friendly cat walker."

"There's nothing to talk about."

"Huh. Not the way I see it."

"I think you have more important matters to be dealing with than my love life."

"I'd rather be a matchmaker or a wedding coordinator at this point. I like happy endings. Wedding tonight?"

There was that ping in Karianne's heart, the one that reminded her happy endings weren't guaranteed. "Heading to my place to get ready."

"Please pray for the night and beyond for the hospital."

"Melissa, you know I haven't prayed since—"

"It doesn't mean you can't start back. God's still there."

"I'll text you later, okay?"

"Sounds good. And if you happen to run into the cat walker again, tell him I said hello." She chuckled, then the call ended.

Karianne shook her head and grinned to herself. What was she going to do with her friend? But Melissa's request ... She meant well, pushing her toward a relationship with Harper and inviting her to pray, the two things she would have wanted years ago. She now struggled with both.

It wasn't that she thought God wasn't there. He was. She knew without a shadow of a doubt He was, but when Ron died, her world stopped. The depth of her soul moaned in grief, and the shattered pieces of her heart still hadn't recovered.

Once at the park, with a full moon confirming she was alone, Karianne unleashed Jake and trudged her way outside the locked fence to the bench. She almost hadn't come with the hour so late, but Jake needed the run and she couldn't help but wonder if Trey Scott was coming as he said.

He was a mystery, and she couldn't pinpoint why. Maybe because he seemed too nice. *That isn't fair*, she reprimanded herself. Harper was also very kind and a perfect gentleman. Yet it wasn't Harper she conjured up so easily when her heart needed a crutch from the past. It was the man with the cat.

Her mind replayed their conversations, the way his mouth lifted at the corners when he smiled, his brown eyes that seemed to darken when he looked at her.

She looked toward Dillon's place. The lights shone in the living room and in the garage. Trey's car was parked in the drive.

If he did come, she'd hint at the fact she wasn't interested in anything more than friendship. It was all she could offer anyone, and it would be wrong not to be upfront from the beginning. She had even mentioned those same feelings to Harper last year. He said he understood, but she expected it was the reason he hadn't returned. Was he hoping with a little time away she'd change her mind?

Karianne looked to Jake, who had found something on the ground that seemed to interest him. He stuck his nose to the grass and jumped back.

"Jake." She laughed. "Whatcha got there, boy?"

He looked at her and barked, then refocused on the ground. He danced side to side and returned his face to the same patch of grass.

The gentle night air caressed her face, and she closed her eyes, welcoming the slightly cooler temperature.

Jake began barking again, and she lazily opened her eyes, expecting to see him still nose deep in turf. Instead, he was barking at a figure walking toward them, which she could only assume to be the man in her thoughts. "Trey."

"I heard Jake from the garage," he said as he neared, Jake now at his legs.

Seeing he was carrying something, she stood to give him a hand. "What do you have there? Need some help?"

"I think I can manage." He did a couple of arm curls with the basket, and his biceps tightened against the sleeve of his shirt. "Unless you're telling me I need to renew my gym membership?"

She shook her head, smiling. "Nah, I think you're good. What's inside?"

"Last time, you mentioned you hadn't eaten. I hope you don't mind. I brought us a snack."

Mind? She was starved. "You really didn't have to go to any trouble. I ate not that long ago." Her stomach groaned as if calling her a liar. Well, she did eat a pack of peanut butter crackers shortly before the wedding.

"No trouble." He walked to the bench she'd occupied and set the picnic basket down. Jake sniffed the contents, his tail wagging like a whip. "I think someone is hungry."

"He's an eatin' machine. Don't mind him."

Trey opened the lid and took out two quart-size plastic bags holding sub sandwiches. "Ham or turkey?"

Was he for real? "This is very kind of you. I … um … Turkey would be good. Thank you."

He handed her the turkey sub and pointed to the basket. "There's bottles of water and individual bottles of sweet tea in here, and for dessert, I brought chocolate chip and macadamia nut cookies. Please help yourself to anything you'd like."

"Thank you," she said again, taking the basket handle.

"You're not stealing the basket, are you? You do plan to share with me?"

"Maybe." She chuckled, setting the basket on the ground where they both could reach its contents. She lowered to the bench and took out her sandwich from the bag.

"It's a nice night. Have you been here long?"

"Not too long. Maybe fifteen minutes or so. Normally after night weddings, I try to give Jake thirty minutes to run around." She took a bite, searching for the dog. She found him rolling on the ground several yards away.

"Does that mean we only have fifteen minutes for my interrogation?"

She grinned, remembering it was his turn to ask her questions. "Nine questions shouldn't take long."

"Then maybe we should play thirty questions?" He took a bite of his sandwich. "I'll start. What's your favorite animal?"

"I'll give you a hint. He's right over there." She nodded in Jake's direction, taking another bite. "This is pretty good," she mumbled around the food in her mouth, forgetting her manners, but he didn't seem to notice.

He took a water from the basket. "I'm glad you like it."

"So tell me, Trey Scott, is your favorite pet a cat?"

"A dog, actually, but I'm not home much. A cat is easier."

"Why do you walk Whiskers?"

"For the same reason you walk Jake. Did you know that in Ohio it's against the law to allow your cat to roam without a leash, even on your own property?"

"No. Wow. I have to admit, I've never seen anyone walk a cat before. The first time I saw you both, I was taken aback."

"I could tell by your smile. Or was it the laughing I heard?"

"Maybe a little of both." She flashed him a grin.

"So how do you know Dillon?"

She cringed inwardly at the question, afraid of where it might lead. "We met here, at the park, the day he was considering buying the property. After he bought the house, I started seeing him in town, and over time, we got to know each other. Helen is a pretty small community."

He took a bite of his sandwich. Several moments ticked by. "Did you and Dillon ever date?"

Why would he ask that? "Me and Dillon? No. Well, yes, we went out a few times, but we soon realized we were better off as friends."

"Does he ever call you Kari?"

Her fingers involuntarily roamed to where her

engagement ring once rested. She looked to her hands and clasped them together. "There are only two people who called me Kari. Dillon is one, and the other was my fiancé."

The water bottle paused halfway to Trey's mouth. "Fiancé?"

"Ron." His name almost stuck coming out. "He … died. Car accident. On our wedding day."

"Karianne …"

She didn't want to go down this road, reliving the past. The alcohol. The abuse. The broken promise he'd change. She traveled it enough on her own, but not now, not here. Not with him. "It was a few years ago." She stood and began looking for Jake. "Come here, boy."

Trey was at her side three steps later. "Please, don't leave."

"I can't stay or … do this. I don't want your pity. And if I hear another person say they're sorry—"

"Let's walk. You don't have to say anything."

"Jake," she called, and he galloped toward her. "I'm tired, Trey. I almost didn't come tonight, but I didn't have your number to let you know."

"You were worried about me, if you didn't show?"

She met his gaze then, uncomfortable with what she'd revealed. She shouldn't care—they were strangers—but for some reason, she did. Jake was sitting at her feet, awaiting his next command.

"Karianne." Trey's voice was soft, gentle. "Walk with me. Jake can come too."

Her body gave a small quiver against the breeze, more

nervous than chill, but when Trey touched her arm, she stilled.

"Hold on." He went to the picnic basket and returned with a small quilt. "I brought it since it was predicted to be a little cooler out than normal." He placed it over her shoulders, his hand grazing her hair.

Her cheeks grew warm at his closeness, and yet she didn't move. "Are you a weather junkie?"

He shrugged, eyes sparkling in the moonlight. "Just making sure the weatherman feels appreciated."

Karianne couldn't find the smile his humor deserved. Silence spread between them, and still standing an arm's touch away, she knew what needed to be said but struggled to find the words.

Trey's gaze intensified. "However this night ends, whether you stay or go, I enjoyed seeing you."

Had he sensed what she was about to say? Either way, he was giving her a way out, and she'd graciously take it. "It was nice. Thank you for dinner."

"I hope to see you again."

"I don't know, Trey. This was sweet and all, but I think you're looking for something I can't give you."

"Your friendship, that's all I'm asking. To have lunch together, maybe dinner, at a restaurant. We both need to eat. Afterward, we can take long walks along the dog park."

She chuckled. "You sound like a dating site. But I prefer long walks along the beach."

"I'm game if you are." He winked, and the corners of his mouth drew into a smile.

Goodness, he was handsome. "I should go." Before she found herself on a beach somewhere.

"Okay, but first I have something for you." He jogged back to the basket and returned with a zip-top bag of cookies. "Here, take this."

She accepted the still-warm bag. "You made these."

His smile widened. The surprise in her voice wasn't lost on him. "Of course." He slipped his wallet from his back pocket and withdrew a business card. "Here's my number. Call or text me anytime."

She looked to the card. *Trey Scott, Co-owner of T & T Construction.* "What's your brother's name?"

"Tate."

"Does the rest of the family's initials start with *T*?"

"You guessed it. Mom's Tessa, and Dad's Timothy."

She removed the quilt and handed it to him. "Thank you again for everything."

"Have a good night."

Jake still sat at her feet, so obedient. She ran a hand down his back. "Come, Jake." He ran in front of her to the Jeep.

No matter how much Karianne wanted to turn around and eat cookies with the man who made them, she kept walking and didn't glance back.

CHAPTER 4

"Dillon, I met Karianne." Trey sat on the couch and pressed the speaker button on his cell.

"I had hoped you might."

He rubbed the bridge of his forehead and let out a small breath. "Until a few days ago, I had no idea she was the same woman you dated. And her fiancé killed himself behind the wheel?" The horror of that was still fresh in Trey's mind.

"Yeah." Dillon's tone was somber. "It happened years after we broke up, but yes, she is the one."

"I've been praying for her since. I wish you would have told me that Kari and Karianne were one and the same. She's still reeling from her loss. If I had known, I would have handled things differently."

"Hmm. Am I wrong to assume you've spent some time together?"

"We've talked at the dog park a couple of times, but last time, I basically asked her out, then backpedaled into friend zone because of the fear in her eyes. I've not seen or heard from her since. She's ... I need your advice."

"Did you have a good time?"

"Yeah, she's beautiful, smart, inquisitive, and has a good sense of humor."

"Give her space. Take it slow. Focus on the fireworks show and see what happens. If this deal goes through, you'll be spending more time in Helen."

"You're right." Trey hadn't come to start a relationship but to grow his business.

"There's something I think you should know. There's a man coming into town named Harper. He's been interested in Kari and made a move at last year's balloon festival, but she wasn't ready. Now, I'm not so sure. I personally think he's wrong for her. Anyway, long story short, Harper is the brother-in-law of her best friend, Melissa, and he might already be in town."

"You know competition is my middle name."

"Then change it. If you want a chance with Kari, patience needs to be your focus. It's the best advice I can give you."

"I hope you don't mind me asking, but I'm trying to put the pieces together. Didn't you and Ron room together in college?"

"After graduation he got a job in Helen, and since I was jobless and needed a place to stay instead of with my parents, I headed there with him. He was the one who met Kari first, but he was seeing someone at the time." Dillon paused. "Ron and I, we were pretty close until the drinking got in the way."

"I'm sorry."

"I don't understand why things happen like they do, and as hard as life is at times, I do know one thing, God is in control. I hold tight to that truth. I miss Ron, but I know one day I'll see him again. Sober. Healed from his addiction. Kari, she lost a part of herself when he died. Maybe even before. I don't know, but the constant in and out of rehabs, the prayers she prayed for him ... nothing ever worked. It all took a toll. I don't know how someone recovers from a relationship with an alcoholic, but losing the person you love a few hours before the wedding ... I can't imagine. I'm afraid she's lost and has forgotten what it means to live."

"Should I back off completely?"

"I don't think you should. Be receptive, patient, but go on with your life. I can't pinpoint why, but I had this feeling in my gut ever since the doors with Helen's city council opened that the two of you should meet." A newborn's cry sounded in the background. "Hey, Trey, I gotta run."

"Tell Lauren I said hello. And congratulations again."

"Will do. Talk to you soon."

Trey ended the call and ran his fingers through his hair. Three days and no word. Was this Harper guy already in town dating her?

He rose from the couch and pocketed his cell. He'd do what Dillon suggested, but first, he'd take Whiskers for a walk. He needed to keep himself busy and finishing another set of racks for the fireworks would do just that.

"Whiskers," he called, unhooking her leash from its hook by the door. She looked up and uncurled herself from her nook in the armchair and arched her back.

"Come on, girl." He jingled the leash, and she perked her ears. "We should get out for a while."

Tail straight up, Whiskers trotted out. Once they were across the street at the dog park, Trey couldn't curb his desire to search Karianne out, or wish for a chance at a moonlit stroll by her side.

"What was I thinking, Melissa? I'm not ready for this." Karianne ran a hand down her blouse trying to press it out. "Let me get my iron."

"I can't even see the wrinkle."

"Look, see here." She pointed to another. "I'll change."

Melissa touched her arm. "Don't. You look great. Why are you so nervous?"

She met Melissa's gaze. "You know why. I haven't been on a date since Ron. What am I supposed to do? Say?"

"It's only Harper."

"Maybe it's not a big deal to you since you're related, but I'm out of my element here." She hurried to the dresser mirror.

"But you know him."

She tucked a strand of hair behind her ear, then studied her profile and smoothed out her powder. "Not really. You know him. Harper coming here for a week last year doesn't count as knowing someone. Ron and I were friends for a couple of years before we started dating. I guess you can say we eased our way into it, and look what happened there." She grabbed her lipstick, applied a thin layer, then pressed her lips together. "Let's talk about something else. What's going on at the hospital? I've been reading the newspaper. Is it true about the hacker?"

"Yes, whoever broke into our system is demanding a ransom. If we pay it, we'll get some kind of decryption key to recover our systems, but from what I understand, it will take months before everything will be back to normal."

Karianne turned and leaned against the dresser. "Really... How much are they wanting?"

"I don't know."

"I never would have imagined."

"At this point, it seems to be the hospital's only option. But whatever they decide, I hope this ends soon to restore normalcy for our patients and staff. The impact of all this has been crippling." Melissa's phone sounded from the corner of the bed. She checked the screen. "Brian and Harper are here. I told him the door was open." She grabbed her purse from the bed and slipped her phone inside. "You don't mind bringing him to the house when you're done?"

"Not at all. Have fun with the in-laws. Don't be out too late."

Melissa shook her head as she left the bedroom, her voice trailing in. "Hey, Harper. She'll be out in a minute. Come on, hon," she said to her husband. "We can't keep your parents waiting."

Karianne took a deep breath as she ambled into the living room. Harper was standing by the window, staring out toward the street, his blond hair longer than she remembered. "Sorry to keep you waiting."

Harper turned, smiling as he went to her. "I just got here." He gave her a hug, his trimmed beard tickling her face. "It's good to see you again." He stepped back, his grey eyes searching her face. "So where are we off to?"

"I know this little restaurant about five miles from here. Bernie's. I made reservations. Interested?"

"Of course. You'd know the best restaurants. It's the reason I asked you to pick the place. Lead the way."

The drive and their effortless conversation to the Nacoochee Valley eased the tension in her shoulders. "The charm, the atmosphere, the food, it brings me back time and time again. I hope you like it." She took the last curve and drove up the drive. "This is it."

"It looks like a B&B."

"Basically, except the restaurant is open to the public." She parked the Jeep and cut the engine. "Our reservation isn't until six. Want to check out the view before we go in?"

"Sounds good," he said exiting the car. "This is wine country, isn't it?"

She hesitated. "It is." They neared a wooden swing that looked out over the valley. She pointed to the view. "That's Sal Mountain."

"Beautiful." He faced her. "While I'm here, why don't we do a wine tour? We can go to different locations, have dinner and sample the wines? What do you say?"

She lowered to the swing, searching for the right words, not wanting to offend him. "I don't drink."

"So, you've never been?"

Not since Ron's death. "I've been to a few wineries. The food is great, but—"

"Wonderful. When would you like to go?"

Did he not catch the part where she wasn't interested in going? "It's not really my thing."

"Eating isn't your thing?"

"Well, yeah, I like to eat, but—"

"We'll have a good time. You don't have to drink."

Anxiety rose to her throat. She took out her phone and checked the time. They still had ten minutes before they could be seated, but she had to move, walk. "Want to see if a table is ready?"

"Sure."

They strolled side by side up the wooden path, uneasiness settling in her stomach. This felt more like a blind date than the friendship they shared getting to know one another last year.

"How have you been?"

She swallowed against the knot caught in her throat. "I've been good." Except for this last week, and now, but he didn't need to know. "I had twelve weddings recently and have seven more before the festival ends."

"How do you keep up? There's a lot that goes into one wedding. I can't imagine so many in such a short time."

"I have a great assistant. I wouldn't give her up for anything."

He held the door for her, and as she entered, the hostess greeted them. "Is the name Karianne?"

"It is. I know we're a little early."

"You're a regular. No problem." She smiled, collecting menus. "Table is ready. Right this way."

The hostess led them through the elegant front room and on to another area just as lovely with its old rustic charm, and seated them in front of the fireplace. The table held water glasses ready to be filled and a vase of fresh-cut purple carnations and yellow roses. "A server will be with you in a moment." She set the menus on the table.

Karianne placed her clutch down on the white linen tablecloth and fingered the rose. "You would think since I'm around flowers most days that I would be tired of them."

"I can see why you like this place. It's nice." He glanced at the menu but eyed the wine and beer list with interest.

She was tempted to lean forward and smell the roses but began to fidget, pressing her hands in her lap. "I'm glad you like it. So what have you been up to?"

"Where to begin? I'm in the process of transferring ownership from one company to another. I enjoy M&A deals."

Karianne had no idea what those were, but the excitement on his face as he spoke for twenty minutes, even during ordering, said she needed to hop on her laptop later tonight and find out. "That's great, Harper. I'm happy for you. Sounds like things are going well."

The hostess came from the kitchen with their plates.

"Not many people can say they love their jobs."

His words triggered thoughts of Trey. If working in the family's business wasn't Trey's dream, what was? "I guess that's true. Not to change the subject, but I've been meaning to ask you, how's Roxy? Melissa told me she had pups."

"She did." He smiled around his bite. "Can you imagine a houseful of golden retrievers? Thankfully, I found homes. I have a few pictures if you'd like to see them?"

"I'd love to."

He lifted the phone from the table, pressed the screen a few times, and handed her the phone. "This first shot is Roxy with her pups. Swipe to the left to see the rest." He took another bite.

"How sweet, Harper. How did you find homes so quickly?" She swiped, seeing Roxy snuggled with two of her babies. The next two photos were the same.

"It seems everyone loves this breed."

"They are beautiful." She continued through the photos, stopping at a picture of Harper with his arm around a woman, each holding up a glass of wine. Her stomach dropped. She flipped back to one of the pup pictures and handed him the phone.

"How's Jake? As nosy as ever?" He chuckled at his own joke, knowing Jake's past and his constant need to sniff things out.

"Of course. What else have you been doing? Besides work?" She cut into her food and took a bite, curious about the pictures she'd seen.

"I did take an unexpected trip. Several coworkers were planning to visit Santa Cruz, Chile, and the famous Clos Apalta Winery. They asked if I was interested in going. Can you believe, at first I said no?

Thankfully, at the last minute I changed my mind. It was a once in a lifetime trip and the best wine I've ever tasted."

Throughout dinner, the conversation continued in the same direction—toward wine, food, and travel. She enjoyed food and experiencing lifetime adventures, but she couldn't see herself part of the life he was describing. Not after Ron. Not again.

Sometime before dessert, Harper grew quiet. Thinking their date was over as they stood to leave, and no more would follow, she invited him to the bench where they started. She'd give him the opportunity to say his piece and move on to the woman in the photo. It was for the best.

"It was nice seeing you again, Karianne."

But ...

"I thought a lot about you since I left."

Really? She tried to hide her surprise.

"Don't look too shocked."

"That obvious, huh?"

"Slightly. I thought about calling you."

"Why didn't you? Friends do talk." Maybe if they had, she'd have a better understanding of who Harper truly was, not who his sister-in-law said he was, or the person her mind pictured the months after he left.

"I wasn't sure I should with how things ended last time, or if you'd be receptive to the idea, but then I started traveling and with work ..."

Last year she was only trying to be open. Had she blown him off as he made it sound? After Ron, she'd admit she was scared when it came to her heart. She never meant to be harsh, but if he thought so, why was he here?

"Harper, I'm not sure what you're saying."

"Karianne, I had to see you. To see if the spark I felt between us was still there."

Had there been a spark? All she remembered was she thought of him often when he left. How he was a gentleman and she thoroughly enjoyed his company.

What could she say? If she was harsh before, she certainly didn't want to seem so again. "I enjoy being with you, but I'm more of a stay-at-home kinda gal who wants to sit with Jake and sip coffee or hot chocolate year round—not wine."

"A couple doesn't always have to enjoy the same things. I could tell wine tasting isn't your thing, but I'd like to share the experience with you." He covered her hand with his.

Ron would agree. They were inseparable and did everything together but drink, though she shared that experience too. She could still taste the alcohol on his tongue and picture the vivid memories of how, drink by drink, the habit stripped the man she loved raw, almost unrecognizable even to her own eyes. She shivered.

She removed her hand from his and stood.

"Karianne, did I say something?" Confusion flittered across his features.

"I thought we could head back to the Jeep. I'm feeling a little chilled."

"Oh, of course." He fell in step with her. "You should have said something."

What would she say, that the past was turning her

insides hollow and any mention of alcohol pricked her skin with fear that she might repeat her mistakes with someone else? That she'd fall in love with a man who chose her second to a drink? Because no matter how much she'd tried to help Ron, she couldn't save him, or anyone else for that matter.

She slowed as they neared the Jeep. "The truth—the reason why I don't drink—my late fiancé, he was an alcoholic."

His brows furrowed as his gaze flicked to hers, then away. "I see."

And that was all that was said before Karianne broke the uncomfortable silence. "I forgot to ask, is Roxy with you?"

"I left her with a friend."

"Too bad. I was hoping she and Jake might connect more this time."

"Like their owners."

The way he was grinning at her … he was a charmer and knew it.

When they reached Melissa's, Harper unlatched his seatbelt and turned to her. "Would you like to come in?"

She looked to the house, and it seemed every light was on. Was she ready to meet Harper's parents and tackle Melissa's questions about the date? "I think I should head home."

"You have off tomorrow."

He had her there. "I know, but I've not been home recently, and I'm sure Jake can use some time out of his crate."

"Are you sure?"

"Yeah, but thank you." She caught the downward turn of his mouth before he moved to open the door. He came around to her side of the Jeep, and she rolled down the window.

"I'll call you."

"Okay."

"I mean it this time. Goodnight."

"Nite, Harper."

He walked up to the porch steps, and as she pulled out of the drive, she caught him in the rearview mirror watching her go.

CHAPTER 5

*E*arly the next morning, Karianne and Jake were at the park, with him sniffing every nook and cranny while she replayed last night's date with Harper. He hadn't called yet, and she was grateful.

Why hadn't Melissa told her about Harper's interest in wine? Maybe she knew she wouldn't give him a chance. If so, she'd been right. Now that Karianne had seen him again, she wasn't sure how to proceed. Was avoidance an option?

No, he'd probably search her out.

Personally, she needed a distraction from the entire mess, but for practicality's sake, she needed to find a way to let Harper know this wasn't going to work. He really was a sweet guy—and nice to look at—but the relationship scared her. She couldn't trust him.

Too bad she wasn't already seeing someone. She looked to Dillon's place for a moment before glancing off in the distance. A little smile lifted her mouth.

She could *pretend* to be seeing someone.

No, she wouldn't lie to Trey. It would be wrong on so many levels. But maybe if she was honest and shared her dilemma with him, he'd help her. They could share that meal he'd mentioned or spend one of the afternoons together at the balloon festival. She just needed enough time for Harper to head back to California.

Her story had to be believable—Melissa would certainly see through her if it wasn't—but not over the top. Just enough for her best friend and her brother-in-law to focus on someone else besides her.

Karianne glanced at her phone. It wasn't yet eight o'clock, but she needed to get home. She had a plan to map out.

She rose from the bench and grabbed her keys. What Trey would say was anyone's guess, but she'd leave the ball in his court.

Had he heard something? Trey hit the pause button on his drill. Silence filled the garage. He waited. Nothing. Taking advantage of the pause, he walked to the kitchen to get water, and heard the doorbell ring.

He chuckled at himself and closed the door into the garage before opening the front door. His smile faded. "Karianne."

"Did I come at a bad time?"

Did she ever. Here was the woman who occupied his thoughts, looking as beautiful as ever, and he hadn't showered or shaved since yesterday. "I've been working in the garage. I didn't hear the doorbell at first."

She pointed over her shoulder. "I saw your car in the drive. I hope you don't mind."

"No. Glad you're here." Though he couldn't understand why. He ran a hand down his scruffy jaw. Why hadn't he at least taken a shower?

"May I come in?"

"Oh, yes. Please." He stepped aside, and as she entered, a hint of vanilla reached him. He closed the door behind her and ushered her into the dining room. "Would you like something to drink? I have tea, water, orange juice. I can make coffee."

She looked to the dining table. "Can we sit?"

"Sure. Is everything all right?"

"It's nothing serious, but I need your help."

Help? "Of course." He pulled out her chair and sat across from her.

She placed her bag on the table and met his gaze. "You might not want to agree until you hear what I'm about to ask."

"I'm listening."

Silence stretched between them. She stood abruptly and paced a few steps, then gripped the back of one of the chairs. "I came up with this plan, but I never imagined how difficult it would be to ask."

He hadn't set eyes on her in over a week. If the plan meant seeing her again sooner than that, he'd do it. Besides, whatever it was, it couldn't be too terrible if she were here to include him. "Please, ask away."

She looked at her hands gripping the chair. "I don't know how long you plan on staying in Helen, but while you're here"—she met his gaze—"will you pretend to be interested in me?"

His heart stopped. Pretend?

"With you being Dillon's friend … and I felt a sense of camaraderie between us …"

She let the words hang, the downward tug of her mouth becoming the defibrillator that jolted him back to his senses. Whatever the reason, he'd accept. "Karianne, please sit. I can tell this is hard for you."

She slowly returned to her seat and fiddled with her pinky nail. "My best friend's brother-in-law, Harper, is in town, and he's interested in a relationship. He's very kind, charming really, but I can't be in his world. I can't do that again. I've thought about this—"

"What can't you do again? Did you date him before?"

"No. No. That's not what I meant." With her nail forgotten, she pressed her fingers together. Her knuckles turned white.

He shouldn't push. Maybe he didn't have the right to know … but she was involving him. "Karianne?"

"Three years ago, on my wedding day, my fiancé died in a car accident after drinking and driving. He drove into a tree. I asked him not to go. Begged him was more like it, and he still went. Always went. No matter what. He said it would be his last drink. Again." She stood and went to the open window. "Some days are still hard, the memories, good and bad. I loved Ron. I'd have given my life for him, but now that he's gone, I can't allow myself to be drawn into that life."

"Why don't you tell Harper that?"

"Because of the other night. When I said I wasn't

interested or comfortable going to a winery, Harper continued to try to persuade me to go. It's not only because of the drinking, but it was like he didn't hear me, though I know he did. Ron did the same, used persuasion to get me to do things I otherwise wouldn't have, and somewhere along the way I lost myself. It's taken me years to see that my relationship with Ron wasn't a healthy one. I can't walk through that door again. It scares me."

He rose, needing a minute to think, but strolled to her side. Karianne was a strong woman, but her relationship with Ron left deep scars, and the wounds had yet to heal. His instinct to comfort her in his arms and protect her from another man hurting her drove him to say yes. And why not? She came to him in need of help. Someone to come alongside her and guide her back to her inherent strength. And he wanted to be the guy to do that.

She was the first to speak. "I thought since you had mentioned going out for dinner, to the park, I could tell my friend and her brother-in-law that I decided to spend time with you. It wouldn't be for long. The festival is a little over a week away. Harper's flight is on the last day. Everything can go back to normal after he leaves."

Trey would have a little over a week for them to get better acquainted, and he'd squeeze in every moment she allowed.

"I shouldn't have asked. I'm not sure what I was thinking." Karianne turned back to the table and reached for her purse.

"I'm in."

She paused mid-grab. "You're in?"

"Yes."

"Are you sure?"

Was he? "If you are."

A small smile lit her face. "Thank you."

Okay. This is happening. "You're welcome. Are you working tomorrow night?"

"In the morning. I'm heading to the warehouse where I buy my flowers. I have five weddings before the festival, so it will be pretty busy."

His time with Karianne was shrinking by the minute. "How does dinner sound? You make reservations wher-ever you'd like, and I'll pick you up at seven."

"Sounds like a plan." Holding her purse strap, she glanced at the door. "I think I should go." She searched a pocket and lifted out keys, then tucked her bag under her arm. "Tomorrow will be a busy day."

"I'm glad you came." He walked her to the foyer and opened the door.

"I am too. Thank you for listening and for your help."

"Anytime." Trey waited until her Jeep rolled down the street before closing the door. Lately, when he'd prayed for a sign where Karianne was concerned, or at least for the opportunity for them to have time together, he'd never pictured her asking him on a date for someone else's benefit.

God must have a sense of humor, because he was getting exactly what he prayed for.

That night, Karianne thought of Trey as she lay in bed. She had texted him her number, but he hadn't replied.

She chuckled, remembering the surprise on his face when he answered the door. But what surprised *her* was his willingness to help. She hadn't meant to go into such personal details about Ron and herself, but now she was glad it had come out. A lot of time had passed since she'd felt comfortable enough to do so—like her words mattered, she mattered—and Trey seemed to accept her for who she was. There wasn't any judgment in his soft brown eyes, only understanding.

Her cell chimed, and she slapped at the nightstand to grab her phone. Harper's number and text appeared on the screen.

Call me when you get a chance. I'd love to see you.

CHAPTER 6

*K*arianne parked in front of the coffee shop and dialed Melissa.

The phone rang several times before she answered. "Hey, stranger. What are you up to today? I've got the day off and can use some girl time after this week at the hospital."

"That would be great, but I have a date tonight … and it's not with Harper." She hated to come right out and say it, but Melissa needed to know before Karianne shared the news with Harper.

"Then with who? I thought your date with Harper went great."

So he must have spoken to her. "It was nice. I do like him, but it seems his interests have changed in the year since I've seen him. I think we'd be better off as friends."

"Why? What happened? What has my brother-in-law gone and done?"

"Oh, Melissa, nothing. It was while we were talking, he shared he's been traveling and enjoying wine tastings, even went to Chile with several coworkers. I know there's nothing wrong with it, but after Ron and everything we went through, I can't take the chance of falling for someone who might have a drinking problem." There was no need to mention his persuasiveness and how uncomfortable it made her feel.

"Karianne, believe me, I had no idea. He's never said anything to me about being a wine aficionado. Brian hasn't mentioned it either. If I'd known …"

"It's all right. I'm glad to find this out now, and I hope you're not upset?"

"Just a little disappointed. Can you blame me? I've dreamt of you being part of my family for years, but I totally understand. After Ron, you can see clearly now, and if Harper isn't the one, he isn't the one."

"Thank you for understanding."

"You haven't told him yet, have you?"

She looked to the car clock. "Not yet. We're meeting in a few minutes. I'm sitting in front of the coffee shop now. Why?"

"He's been planning something. Brian mentioned something about … what was it about the festival?"

Harper pulled into an empty spot a few spaces down from her and parked.

"Hey, he's here. You keep thinking and I'll call you later."

"Yes, and I need to hear about this mystery date, though I have a feeling I know who it's with."

Karianne unlatched her seatbelt as Harper, looking handsome in jeans and a slim-fit beige button-down shirt, strolled to the store front.

"Have fun tonight."

Karianne ended the call and with a heavy breath, left her Jeep and followed him inside. She wasn't as nicely dressed in her black leggings and royal blue tee, which she'd grabbed off the clearance rack at one of her favorite stores, but she was here.

He smiled as soon as he saw her. "Hi there." Placing an arm around her shoulders, he kissed the top of her head. His movements were fluid, as if this was their natural greeting. "How are you this morning? What would you like to order?" He turned his attention to the chalkboard menu hanging from the wall.

She, on the other hand, was taken off guard by the display of affection. Memories from the year before began filling her thoughts. The way Harper held her hand that last night under the stars. The way her heart rose and fell when he looked at her. She'd been wrong earlier. There had been something between them. There had been a spark, and her thoughts pined after him when he left. Week after week, she'd waited for a call, but nothing. She took it as a sign she was finally opening herself up to love, but Harper wasn't the one. She never expected the affection. "Carmel chocolate. Medium."

His focus shifted to the cashier. "I'd like a Pikes Peak, large, a Carmel Chocolate, medium, and two Danishes. One cream cheese. One cherry."

He remembered she liked the cream cheese Danishes. Not good.

When their order arrived, she scanned the café and decided she liked the look of the empty circular table near the door. Secluded enough for others not to overhear.

"This is a cozy spot," he said, setting their order on the table to his left. A little nook, perfect for two. Shoot.

She sat down and Harper served her. "Still like cream cheese, I hope." He smiled as he sat across from her. "How's your morning been so far?"

"Uneventful, which I don't mind. My assistant and I will be hauling flowers from the warehouse today and will finish decorating the venue for the wedding tomorrow." She took a bite of her Danish and almost moaned. "I've been so busy, the last time I had one of these was about three months ago. Thank you."

"Welcome. I'm glad you're enjoying it." He finished off his Danish in two bites and wiped his bearded mouth with a napkin.

She sipped her coffee, enjoying the warmth. Her body relaxed for the first time since she walked through the door.

"And I'm glad to see you this morning."

She cupped her hands around the coffee cup. How was she going to break this off? "Harper, we need to talk."

"Hey, Karianne."

She looked up to find Trey, breathtakingly handsome in a navy blue suit, strolling toward their table. She fought to get her voice working. "Hi," she finally squeaked. She had nothing to feel guilty about, but somehow she did. "Let me introduce you to my friend Harper. Harper, this is Trey."

Harper stood and held out his hand. "A friend of Karianne's?"

Trey returned the greeting. "Something like that. Nice to meet you." He looked to the counter, then met her gaze. "I was going to call you. I'm meeting with the city council for most of the day, so if you call and I don't answer right away, you'll know why."

"Trey," the cashier called, holding up his coffee order.

"Nice to meet you, Harper." Trey nodded. "Karianne, we're still on for tonight?"

"Unless something comes up on your end."

"Not a chance. See you at seven." He hurried to the counter and then dashed out of the café without a backward glance.

A lump lodged in Karianne's throat when she thought of what she was about to do. If she didn't, would Harper push her into a relationship as he tried the other night about wine tasting? Moments ticked by before Harper lifted his coffee and took a sip.

"I was planning to tell you."

"Right before he walked in?"

"I was."

"I had a feeling you were going to say something important." He took another sip and set his cup down.

"I'm sorry, Harper." She tried to watch for a reaction, to read him, but came up blank. He was watching her. Karianne's face must have registered the truth because he shot her a smile.

"So tell me about Trey. How long have you been dating? Melissa didn't mention anything."

Karianne stared into the distance, gaze trying to find

a spot to land. She was regretting not telling him the truth, but would Harper laugh at her, embarrass her for the way she felt as Ron had? "It's probably because we aren't dating, really, officially. We're ... taking it slow." *Stop babbling, Karianne.* "We see each other several times a week."

"What you're saying is I have a shot."

She froze at the determined gleam in his hazel eyes. "Harper ..."

"I know. I know. You and Trey are kinda dating, not really, but seeing each other. Sounds to me you're not sure about him or the relationship."

She didn't know what this was, but he seemed assertive suddenly. Could she stand up for herself? She sat up, trying to appear confident. "I didn't say I was unsure."

"So what *would* you say?"

"That I enjoy his company. We have a good time together."

"Like us."

She leaned forward. "This is different, him and I." *But is it really? You can't know someone within a week's time.*

Harper rose from his chair, gathering their trash.

"Where are you going?"

His mouth tightened slightly. "I don't want to hold you up. You've got a busy day." He threw away their trash and grabbed his coffee.

Once they reached the curb, she slowed as awkwardness settled between them. "Thank you for breakfast. Please tell your family good-bye for me."

"You can tell them Friday night. We have a dinner

date, remember? It's already planned. The entire family is coming."

She met his gaze, trying to figure him out. "We never actually set a date. I hadn't gotten back to you. Besides, as I mentioned, I'm seeing someone," she said with more conviction this time.

"Are you? Because my first impression is that Trey seems like a man who's more interested in his meeting with the city than his girlfriend having lunch with another man."

Karianne eyed a yellow convertible driving by. Of course, he was right. Trey had only agreed to help her out because of her desperation. If Harper could see through the façade, what difference did it make if he saw her with Trey? "I'll have to let you know."

He tucked a few strands behind her ear, his fingers lingering along her hair. "You're worth fighting for, Karianne." A smile lightened his face. "I'll call you tonight."

Unable to describe the feelings wrapping her stomach into knots, she ambled blindly to her vehicle, trying to pinpoint the emotions tripping her heart and brain. But she needed to think clearly about what to do next.

CHAPTER 7

*T*rey grabbed his keys from the kitchen bar and caught sight of Whiskers eyeing him from the food bowl.

"Sorry. I haven't given you much attention today, have I? Too much on my mind." He went to the pantry and grabbed the bag of dry cat food, then squatted and dumped some in the bowl. "Forgive me?" He stroked her back a few times as she ate. "You know that dog owner? We're going out tonight. Maybe you and Jake could meet. Karianne and I have talked about it." After standing, he returned the food to the pantry.

Who was he kidding? When was the last time he'd heard of a cat and dog getting along? If his recent visit to the vet with Whiskers in tow was any sign of the future, it might be best to keep Jake far away. But Jake seemed like a well-behaved dog. Karianne had obviously trained him well. Hopefully, the outcome would work out for them all. "See ya, girl."

Ten minutes later, Trey pulled in to Karianne's drive.

Before he could get out, the front door opened and the woman of his thoughts stepped out. She wore a short-sleeve, light-blue dress that tied at her waist and hung just above the knee. Underdressed in jeans and a button-down shirt, he hurried to the passenger side door and opened it while she locked up.

"Hi," he said when she neared. Should he compliment her on how beautiful she looked? Or just keep it to himself? Captivated by the way her eyes seem to brighten when she looked at him, he said nothing.

"Hi."

They stood so close, with her vanilla scent tantalizing him, that it took him a moment to remember what he'd been planning to say. "Where are we off to?"

"Cowboys and Angels. They have great food, and their courtyard is beautiful this time of year."

"Sounds perfect. Lead the way."

She slid in, and he closed the door behind her. How did you tell a woman you'd just met that she was the one you were going to marry one day? He sent up a quick prayer for wisdom and patience as he strolled to the driver's side door.

Karianne gave the restaurant's address, and as they drove off, she focused out the window.

He glanced at her. She seemed quiet, didn't she? Should he ask? "I haven't known you very long, but I can tell when something is bothering you," he said, anxious by what she might say next, especially if it concerned him. "Would you like to share?"

"I appreciate you agreeing to go out with me, but after tonight, it's really not necessary."

Hmm. What had happened with Harper to change her mind? *Lord, I need that wisdom.* "What changed?"

"This morning, I realized we weren't really fooling anyone, especially Harper."

"How do you figure?"

"He made a comment that got me thinking. If we were really seeing each other, you would've been more interested in Harper and me having breakfast together."

Oh, he was interested all right. It was the reason he made a point to introduce himself to Harper and imply his relationship with Karianne was more than friendship. Trey couldn't have been any clearer about his interests—unless he'd kissed her right then and there. Perhaps he should have for Karianne's sake, so she'd know his true intentions, but to a man like Harper, Trey had claimed Karianne loud and clear.

"I didn't help matters when I mentioned we weren't officially seeing each other. He proceeded to tell me that I must not be sure about you or our relationship, and about how he still has a shot."

"Does he? I mean, are you interested in seeing him again?"

"I was." She took a heavy breath and continued. "Last year when I met Harper, it was nice. It was the first time in years that I started to rethink the future. It was also the first time I allowed myself to enjoy another man's company. I knew my heart would soon be ready to let someone in, it just wasn't the right time. I shared my feelings with Harper the night of the festival, but after he returned home, he never called."

"Not once?"

"No. I didn't even know he was going to be in town until Melissa said he was coming. He seems different than before, and that brings us back to why we're on this date."

Trey pulled in to the restaurant parking lot, parked, and turned the car off, but neither of them moved. "Do you want my advice?"

"Please."

"I think we should continue with what we agreed to do, but for this to look real, it needs to be real. We'll spend quality time together up until the moment he catches his flight. Maybe if he sees us together, he'll understand you're unavailable."

Her eyes widened, hopeful. "Do you think we can still make this work?"

The tension in his shoulders relaxed. "I do. So, what do you say about starting our date out right with a great meal? I'm starving."

She chuckled. "As you say, I'm in."

"Good. I'm coming around for you." He got out and hurried around to her side, then opened the door.

"Thank you, kind sir."

"Anything for you." He gave a slight bow, and a pink hue tinted her cheeks as she stepped from the car. He held out his elbow to her, and after a brief hesitation, she took his arm.

A canopy of white lights hung across the restaurant's courtyard, lighting the darkening sky. A line of tables topped with flowers led to the restaurant's entrance.

Karianne slowed. "Isn't it beautiful? I just love the lanterns and flowers. Do you mind if we eat out here?"

She looked up at him, amber eyes expectant, searching his.

How could he say no to her with the way she looked at him? "Wherever you like." They found an unoccupied table near the walkway to the restaurant, and Trey pulled out her chair and then sat across from her. "What do you suggest?" He picked up his menu.

"The Cowboy Ribeye is great, but so is the Classic Charleston Style Shrimp and Grits. You can't go wrong with either."

"Then I'll take your word for it and go with the ribeye."

She leaned forward. "When we're out, please don't feel obligated to pay for me."

"For this to look real, it needs to be real. Besides, can you imagine what my mom would say if she discovered I took a woman on a date and had her pay? She'd have a few choice words for me. You're not going to let that happen, are you?"

She chuckled. "I guess not. I'll have to make it up to you then."

"Whiskers needs a bath."

"Not on your life, Cat Walker."

The laughter in her eyes warmed him inside. *Lord, I need that patience right about now. Please make the fireworks show a success. This is where I belong.*

After Trey ordered, he observed Karianne, how she spoke with her hands and how small they were, the way strands of her hair continued to graze the side of her mouth no matter how many times she tucked them behind her ear. He imagined the softness of her hair.

She took a sip of her water and smiled. "What? The way you're looking at me …"

How was he looking at her? Probably like a lost puppy who'd found a home. "I think Jake and Whiskers need to meet. We've talked about it before, but I think it's time."

"I'd like that. I work tomorrow, so how about Friday? Oh, wait. Friday isn't a good day. It seems I have an obligation I didn't know about. Harper made plans for us with his family."

"Karianne, you don't have to go if you don't want to. Did you accept?"

"I told him I'd let him know."

"We can make plans, and you can give your regrets." He shrugged. "I don't mind being your scapegoat."

The smile returned. "I think I'm going to like having you around."

"That settles it."

"What does?"

"That we're official."

Four hours later, after closing the restaurant down and heading home, Trey glanced at Karianne in the passenger's seat with her head resting back. Her eyes were closed, and a sweet expression settled on her features.

He sighed inwardly. He would have stayed all night if they hadn't needed to leave, and it seemed like Karianne might have agreed. Although now, as the streetlights showed how tired she was, he didn't regret a moment they were together. He'd enjoyed the banter between them, how many times they seemed to know what the other was thinking, and how her laugh warmed his heart. "Are you sleeping?"

"No, just resting."

"That basically means you're asleep."

"Then you won't hold my sleep talking against me, will you?"

"Never. Well, it depends on what you say."

"I had a great time tonight." She opened her eyes and smiled.

"So did I. Which leads me to ask, would you be interested in bringing Jake to my place after work tomorrow night so he can meet Whiskers? I can make dinner. I know you'll be hungry."

"Trey, you don't have to go to all that trouble. I can bring Jake, but you don't have to cook."

"Of course I do. I have to eat too. Do you like Italian?"

"Yes, but—"

"No, buts. If you're coming, I'm cooking. Can you imagine what my mom would say if she knew I asked you over and didn't cook? She'd be ashamed."

She chuckled. "Do you always worry about what your mom would think?"

"When you have an Italian mother who engraved into you since you were five how to treat a woman, you do what you've been taught, even as an adult."

She straightened in her seat. "You're Italian? You don't sound Italian."

"No, but I look more Italian than my brother. He takes after Dad, whereas I take after Mom."

"So you're wanting to make me an authentic Italian meal?"

"That's the plan."

"Huh."

"Is that a good *huh* or a bad *huh*?"

"You've surprised me, is all."

"That's good, right?"

She didn't answer that. "Thank you. I'm happy to accept your invitation. I might not be done until six or a little after. By the time I get home, change, and grab Jake, it might be closer to seven."

"Sounds perfect. You'll be done earlier than I was expecting. Seven or eight will work." He pulled into her driveway and put the car in park. "Let me walk you to the door." Once at her doorstep, silence ensued. He wanted to speak, say something, but didn't know where to start.

Karianne broke the stillness. "If I'm running late tomorrow, I'll let you know."

"That would be great." Another moment ticked by before she turned and unlocked the door. His heart raced. Was this a good idea? "Karianne."

She turned.

She's not ready for a relationship. You'll push her away. "See you tomorrow." With that, he took the porch steps two at a time and headed back to the car.

Patience. Lord, I need your patience.

CHAPTER 8

With a satisfied breath, Karianne watched as the bride and groom swayed on the dance floor. How they held each other close, how intimate they seemed in the moment, their smiles … She wanted this, to love and be loved again. Longing found its way to her heart, bringing Trey to mind.

She didn't know him, yet when they stood on her doorstep after their perfect evening, she wanted their date to be real. She wanted something that was impossible, that his current city construction project—whatever it was —would become a permanent job so he'd still be here after the festival was over. No man had ever cooked a meal for her. It was bad enough when he brought her a picnic basket full of food to the park, especially the warm cookies he baked himself. It would do her well to remember, when they were together tonight eating his Italian cooking, that he would be going back to his life in Ohio.

"Karianne, the bride and groom are about to leave."

Betsy announced, coming toward her. "The baskets of bubbles have been handed out. They're circulating now."

She checked her watch. "Right on time. The limo is here and their bags are loaded." She took a final look around before meeting Betsy's keen gaze. "Another successful wedding. Thank you. I couldn't do this without you."

"We couldn't do this without each other. Two more before the festival. We've got this."

Karianne smiled at her assistant. Always the encourager. "We do, don't we?"

"Absolutely."

Three hours later, Karianne rang Trey's doorbell, holding Jake's leash. "You be a good boy, especially around Whiskers." She leaned down close to his ear. "Please don't kill her."

The front door swung open, and Trey gave a wide grin. "Come on in. Dinner is almost ready."

"Oh, what are we having?"

Trey shut the door behind Jake, who sniffed the air, and led them to the kitchen. "Chicken marsala." He grabbed the pan's handle and gave it a quick jerk, then nabbed a wooden spoon from the counter. "I hope you like mushrooms."

"I do." She set her purse on the bar stool and went to the stove, leaning in as he stirred the chicken and mushroom contents. "Looks great. Smells great too." She took a step back when Jake pushed forward to see the food for himself. "Jake thinks so too."

He chuckled. "Once this is finished, we'll be ready to

eat. And you don't have to leave him leashed." He nodded to Jake.

She glanced around. "Where's Whiskers?"

"Somewhere around here. She can take care of herself."

Karianne wasn't so sure, but that was one of the reasons she was here, for their pets. She unhooked the leash from his collar and stuffed it into her purse. "Can I do anything?"

"Do you mind setting the table? The plates are to my right."

She opened the cabinet, withdrew two plates, and carried them to the dining room. The long, bare table stopped her in her tracks. Jake halted at her feet. "It's just the two of us," she whispered, suddenly anxious.

Jake's head tilted.

"Not us, boy. Trey and I." Deciding to give Trey the head of the table, she set her plate to his left. She and Jake reentered the kitchen to grab glasses, which already waited on the counter with ice. "What would you like to drink?" She opened the fridge.

"Whatever you'd like. I'm not picky." Trey carried the pan of chicken marsala into the dining room.

Water it was. She filled their glasses.

Trey came back through and opened the oven. Out came a dish of asparagus and then another of mashed potatoes.

"Wow, everything looks and smells wonderful."

"I hope you like it. It seems I have Jake's approval."

She followed Trey into the dining room and set the

glasses on the table. "What can I say. We're easy to please."

He touched her arm. "You sit. I forgot something."

When he left, Karianne pointed to a spot next to her chair. "Down, Jake."

Jake obeyed, and as she sat, Trey returned with silverware and napkins.

"Before we dig in, do you mind if we offer a blessing?"

"That's fine. I don't mind."

A smile lit his face, and an odd flutter found its way to her middle, but it only grew when he held out his hand for hers. Distracted by his touch, she barely caught his prayer.

"...thank you for this meal and for allowing me to share it with Karianne. Thank you for always providing. In Your name, amen."

"Amen," she breathed, the word tripping her heart.

He didn't release her hand. "Everything all right?"

He noticed? "I ... I haven't prayed in some time."

"Because of what happened with Ron?"

A few seconds ticked by as she considered her answer. "We used to pray together before... It feels odd ... praying with you. Holding your hand."

"Is it uncomfortable?"

She looked at their joined hands. "Praying ... yes. Holding your hand?" She wouldn't dare tell him how right it felt. "No."

He ran his thumb over her knuckles. "This is me, Karianne. There's no pretense. No deep, dark secrets, only a man who loves the Lord and wants to follow Him."

At a loss for words in the emotion of the moment, she didn't know how to respond, other than to reclaim her hand and say the obvious. "Maybe we should eat. The food is getting cold."

"Good idea. Let's hope not too cold." He scooped chicken onto her lifted plate and then placed some on his own. Steam rose from the pan.

Once she added the sides and set her plate down, she cut into the chicken. At first bite, a moan escaped her throat. "Wow, Trey. This is wonderful. Really."

He took his own bite. "I'm glad you like it. Thankfully, it's still warm."

"It's perfect. Even the garlic mashed potatoes."

Trey looked to Jake. "He's so well behaved. You've taught him well."

"Actually, I didn't train him. I'm not sure who trained him, but he's retired from the service."

"Really? What kind of service?"

"Army. His handler is still in the field. Jake was showing signs of PTSD, so they retired him."

Trey gave such a thoughtful glance at Jake that she almost asked what he was thinking. "Jake's pretty special, then," he said.

"He is. He's helped and saved so many lives ... including mine. I don't know what I would have done without him."

"I believe God knew what you were going through after Ron, so He sent Jake to you."

Karianne took several bites, thinking about that. Had God sent Jake? Without a doubt. She had received Jake right after Ron's funeral, when she needed him most. "I believe you're right. I hope one day Jake can be reunited with his handler. Maybe God will allow it, knowing what his handler has been through, and I'm certain he misses him."

"I'm sure he does."

Jake barked and then growled, but stayed where he lay.

"Whiskers," Trey called. "You must be here."

Whiskers jumped up onto the chair next to Trey and glanced at Jake as he continued to bark.

"It's fine, boy," she said in a soft voice, one that seemed to calm him at times. She leaned over and petted his head.

He quieted and Whiskers stretched out across the chair's cushion.

"It seems their first meeting was a success." Trey took a bite and winked. "Next is dessert."

Trey could cook a mean dinner, but his dessert-making skills were lacking. Fortunately, the local bakery had a chocolate pie Karianne loved, which he knew thanks to a conversation with Betsy. Of course, it was their little secret. He'd have gone to any length to make sure the night was a success. Their pets were another matter altogether. Rarely were archenemies in the animal kingdom friends. However, he knew the Creator of all things, and prayed for peace between them for every-one's sake.

Trey cut up the pie and took two plates into the living

room. As he handed one to Karianne, the fork slid off the plate. She grabbed it.

"Nice catch." He grinned.

"Softball skills."

"You played?"

"Yep. Can you guess the position?"

He sat on the couch next to her. "Mmm … catcher."

"High school and college. Those were the days." She took a bite. "Mmm. This is my favorite."

"Then I did good?" He relished that smile of hers, and the joy radiating from her face. What he wouldn't do to be the man who put that light in her eyes day after day. For her to know that he could be trusted, especially with her heart.

"You did. The entire evening has been wonderful. Do you always try to impress your make-believe girlfriends?"

"No. Only one. You."

She tipped her head, her smile fading as she ate another bite of pie.

"Did I say something wrong?"

Her gaze shifted to Jake lying near her feet. "You caught me by surprise."

"When we're together, Karianne, it feels natural."

She sat up straighter and cleared her throat. "So you've never cooked for anyone else?"

"I've cooked for my family, but besides them you're the first."

Whiskers crossed the living room, eyeing Jake near the couch. As she crept by him, he barked, and Whiskers jumped in midair before bolting toward the bedroom hallway. Jake made chase.

Karianne rushed to her feet and set her plate on the coffee table before running after them. "Jake! Leave that poor kitty alone."

Trey followed. Entering his bedroom, he found Karianne on her knees and leaning under the queen bed, calling Whiskers. She dropped the tan bed skirt and turned to him. Pink tinted her cheeks. "She looks afraid. I'm so sorry."

Jake darted to the left, then to the right. He stuck his nose under the bed and barked.

Trey moved closer. "I don't think he's trying to hurt her. He looks like he wants to play."

"Tell that to Whiskers." She grabbed Jake's collar. "Heel."

Jake obeyed, sitting in perfect stillness, but his eyes stayed trained on the bed.

"I think we should go."

"You don't need to leave."

She looked at Jake and exhaled. "I think we do. Come, Jake." She released him, and he followed without hesitation to her Jeep. After placing her things in the backseat, she escorted Jake in and shut the door behind him.

Trey opened the driver's door for Karianne, but this wasn't how he wanted the night to end. "What are your plans for tomorrow? Will you have dinner with Harper and his family?"

She looked to him. "I haven't decided."

"I meant what I said before."

"About you being my scapegoat?"

"Yes, and about this pretend relationship being real."

As he collected her hands in his and met her gaze, she said nothing. "Whatever you decide about Harper, it's up to you, but know I'm here."

She swallowed. "Trey."

"Just think about it." He released her hands. "Tomorrow morning, I'll be taking Whiskers to the pet store and then for a walk. If you'd like to join us, we'll be leaving about ten."

She nodded and climbed into the driver's seat, but it didn't seem like an agreement. "Thank you again for tonight. I had a wonderful time."

"You're so welcome."

Later that night as Trey drudged his way through loading the dishwasher, he was tempted to pick up the phone and dial Karianne, but held back. He'd made his intentions clear. Now he'd have to wait to see if she and Jake would join them.

CHAPTER 9

The next morning Karianne wrestled over decisions about Harper and Trey. Harper felt like an obligation she couldn't shake, but with Trey, she thoroughly enjoyed their time together. The way he made her smile. The way he listened when she spoke. Or how he made dinner last night and surprised her with her favorite cake. However he found out, it was just another reason she was taken by him. She wasn't used to someone caring enough to discover her likes and dislikes, taking the time to figure out who she was on the inside.

Oh, how hard it was not to think of Trey, and how even more difficult to walk away last night when she wasn't ready to go. She couldn't stop thinking of the way he held her hands, gentle yet strong. The way he made her feel as if she'd be safe by his side.

Time and time again, his words replayed in her thoughts.

Only one. You.

When we're together, Karianne, it feels natural.

…this pretend relationship being real.

Was he serious?

Down deep she knew. There was no question. He wanted to date her. A real relationship. Her heart began to race.

This was really happening.

Karianne checked her watch. Quarter till nine. She had to hurry if she planned to meet Trey. Her stomach churned with excitement as she rushed to ready herself and Jake. Trey had told her to think about them starting a real relationship. She was finally ready to move forward with her life, and she couldn't wait to tell Trey. How she longed to love someone again. Someone she could trust.

Karianne pulled into Trey's driveway fifteen minutes early and led Jake up the steps to the front door.

The door swung open soon after she'd rung the bell. His surprised expression made her smile. *He didn't think I would come. Well, it won't be the only surprise today.* "Hi."

"You came."

"I did."

He smiled at that, then glanced around. "I can't find my keys anywhere."

"Do you want me to drive?"

"Either way is fine, but I still need to lock up. Give me a minute or so. I know they're around here somewhere." Trey strolled toward his bedroom while she and Jake hung out in the foyer. Whiskers cried in the distance, drawing her and Jake's attention.

"Don't you dare, boy. I don't need you messing things up right now."

A sorrowful kitty moan pulled at Karianne's heart, so

she ordered Jake to stay where he sat and went to find Whiskers. The carrier was in the kitchen near the garage door, which was partially open.

She knelt, sticking her fingers through the metal bars. "Hey, girl."

Whiskers moaned once again, and Jake was by her side within moments. Then he pushed his way past her into the garage.

"Jake. This isn't your house." She stood and followed Jake into the garage. Her heart gave way as Jake stood stoic next to black tubes mounted on boards with wires snaked every which way connecting to one another.

Her heart couldn't perceive what her mind told her. The sheer number of … Her brain refused to believe it. Jake hadn't moved but sat still as death, naming it for her.

Bombs.

Oh, Lord. What do I do?

She glanced around, panic setting in as her eyes caught the gravity of the situation. Explosives lined every shelf.

She yanked Jake's collar. "Come, Jake. We have to go." She couldn't think. Her mind blanked out, refused her the words to release him from where he stood. "Please. Jake." Tears filled her eyes as Trey's voice grew close.

"Karianne?" Trey now stood behind her, and her blood ran cold, lightheadedness overtaking her. "What are you doing in here?"

She tugged on Jake's collar once again. He wouldn't budge.

"Jake can't be in here. It's not safe."

"Really. You think?" she shouted.

Trey looked at her oddly, but she didn't care.

"I thought you were different. You said no secrets. I'm so gullible to men. I shouldn't have trusted you." She wobbled slightly.

Trey caught her by the arm. "Karianne, are you all right?"

Her name. His touch sent her reeling back into the house and out the front door to her car. She had to call the police. Reaching for her cell in the console, Karianne caught sight of Trey coming toward her.

"It wasn't a secret," he said, "but more of a surprise."

"Oh, it's a surprise all right. The police will think so too."

"Police?"

She quickly dialed 911. The operator answered immediately, but Karianne broke in. "There are bombs. Shelves full in the garage."

"Bombs?" Trey grabbed the phone and spoke into it. "There are no bombs. They're fireworks for the festival. It's all a misunderstanding."

"Sir," she heard faintly through the phone still pressed to Trey's ear, "we have no choice but to investigate. What is your address?"

Trey's face fell, and his jaw tightened as he gave the address.

Fireworks? Why would he be making fireworks for the festival? He could be lying.

After the call ended, Trey ran his fingers through his

hair. "This isn't good," he murmured as he wandered back to the house.

Karianne was confused. What was going on? Was he telling the truth? Or Jake? She wanted answers but decided to wait for the police. Yet it wasn't only the police that arrived. Unmarked black SUVs soon blocked off the street.

～

If it weren't for the ache in the center of his back and his numb limbs, Trey would have thought he was having an out-of-body experience. His mind tried to comprehend the last seven hours and how he'd found himself snared like an animal.

He shifted in the metal chair, his thoughts finding their way to Karianne once again. How she thought so little of him turned his stomach. What had Ron done to cause her to harbor such distrust? Was she so lost to Trey that they had no hope for the future? Had he been wrong in thinking that the Lord was in their relationship?

Learning that Jake was a bomb dog while being interrogated by both the police and FBI came as a surprise. Why hadn't she shared that information with him when she mentioned Jake was a retired service dog? If she had, he could have explained there was a common ingredient in bombs and fireworks which is why Jake tagged his tubes in the garage.

Trey glanced down at his hands. He'd heard the FBI was in town working on another case, but being in their custody was something he'd never imagined would happen to him. At least he wasn't fingerprinted and booked, but the straight faces he encountered reassured him nothing was taken off the table. He'd given them everything they wanted and more. From his emails with the city council about the festival to his shipments from Ohio. Nothing seemed to help his case. He prayed that whatever happened didn't shine a negative light on his companies, or on the town of Helen. He couldn't lose the respect of his customers in Ohio or his business with the city.

The door swung open and two men—one tall, the other short—stood around him. "Mr. Scott. It seems your statements have been confirmed by the members of the city council. Since your paperwork is all in order, you're free to go."

Trey closed his eyes and felt a hitch in his throat. He'd never once been in trouble with the law, not even for a parking citation, and here was the FBI telling him he was free to go.

He stood on shaky legs. "What about the fireworks?"

"They're being held in a facility the city deemed appropriate since they were removed from the residence."

The taller man, who'd hardly spoken through the whole process, handed over Trey's belongings. "We're sorry for keeping you so long, but with what happened at the hospital, we needed to make sure you weren't connected in some way."

Several questions they'd asked were now starting to make sense. "I appreciate you both making sure people are safe." But as he grabbed his things from the table, he couldn't wait to leave.

Once he pushed through the double doors and exited the station, he recalled how the police had brought him in. His car still sat in the driveway at Dillon's residence. He pulled his cell from the plastic bag and was searching for a taxi when he heard his name. The sight of Karianne made him wince, but as she neared and he looked into her glossy eyes, his heart softened.

She stopped a few feet away. "Do you need a ride?"

"I guess I do."

"I'm … I'm parked right over there." She pointed. "By the nearest police vehicle."

It was only a ten-minute drive to Dillon's place, but the invisible wall between them made the trip seem like an eternity.

"Trey, we need to talk." Karianne was the first to break the silence. "I have—"

"I'm too exhausted tonight, but soon. Maybe tomorrow?"

"Tomorrow I have weddings back-to-back."

When she pulled into the driveway and parked, Trey opened the door. "Then maybe the day after. Thanks for the ride." He got out and closed the door without waiting for a response. As tired as he was, if he said much more, he wasn't sure how his words would be perceived.

Inside, he found overturned couch pillows. The mail had been opened. Other things had been moved. He'd need to tell Dillon the place had been searched.

Later, as he lay in bed fighting for sleep against the horror of the day, his cell phone lit in the darkness. He reached over and grabbed it.

I tried to tell you earlier, but it couldn't wait. I'm so sorry.

He stared at the text.

He needed time.

Everything he'd dreamt, even prayed for over the years, had been coming into fruition, and now he might lose it all.

CHAPTER 10

"We did it," Betsy said as she turned off the reception hall lights. "We've never had four weddings on the same day. I was a bit concerned when you told me about the added weddings, but we did it. What are you going to do with your two weeks off before the next one?"

What was Karianne going to do? With her heart in such a mess over Trey, she hadn't thought that far ahead. Hadn't expected a man to walk into her life like he had, or at all. To make matters worse, he'd been nothing but kind to her and look at what she'd done. Gotten him arrested.

"Hey, are you all right? You're quieter than usual." Betsy stared at her as she stood holding the door open.

How long had she been standing there? "I'm fine. And I'm not sure what I'm going to do yet." Karianne pulled her keys from her clutch as they stepped outside, then turned and locked the door.

"I have an idea." Betsy flashed her a smile as they

strolled to their cars. "I bet if you asked Trey to stay a little while longer, he would."

Her words brought such an ache to Karianne's heart that her steps slowed. She'd put all her focus on today's weddings, but now that they were over, the reality of last night hit her hard. Trey wouldn't stay for her. There was just no coming back from what she'd done. She picked up the pace and headed for her Jeep. "Night, Betsy. See you at the festival."

"See you then."

Karianne had been home less than five minutes when she called Melissa.

Last night, after receiving no response to her text to Trey, Karianne had broken down and spilled everything to Melissa. From Harper's pushiness to Trey agreeing to date her, to the unexpected feelings Trey stirred, to calling the police on the man she was falling for, to her deep-rooted fear of trusting another human being like she had Ron.

When Melissa's voicemail picked up, Karianne ended the call without leaving a message.

A knock sounded at the door. Jake jumped from his bed and barked, running to the door.

Trey. She hurried to answer, only to find Melissa holding a half-gallon of mint chocolate chip ice cream in one hand and rocky road in the other.

"I came prepared."

Inhaling a deep breath of regret, she ushered her friend in. "I just called you."

"I know. How are you doing?" Melissa walked into the kitchen and set the ice cream containers on the counter.

"Confused. Upset at myself. He hasn't called."

"You really like him, don't you?"

"I know it's crazy. We've only just met weeks ago, but the kindness in his eyes draws me. He's thoughtful, and he makes me feel safe when we're together."

"Can I tell you how surprised I am to hear you talk about someone without being skeptical?"

"Yeah, but what does it matter now? I've lost him, and I know it. I caused this. Ron used to say——"

"It doesn't matter what Ron used to say or what Trey does. What matters is what God says. He loves you just the way you are, regardless of what other people say or think. He's not going to let you go, whether you trust Him or not."

She wanted it to be true. To be loved that way. But … "I've messed things up."

"You aren't responsible for Ron's actions."

She could agree with that. "But what about my own? I walked away from God and allowed Ron to take His place. I lied to Harper and used Trey, all things I hate, and all because I was too afraid to voice my feelings."

"The Lord sees your mistakes and bad choices, but He offers grace."

"But I can't even trust myself to make good decisions. Once I saw Jake standing beside the fireworks, which I thought were bombs, I lost it. I couldn't think about anything else but being trapped in another man's lies."

"Nothing that happened with Trey surprised the Lord. I know it's hard to trust after Ron, but I think it's time you trust in God. Maybe Trey."

Could she trust God enough to give Him everything that happened between her and Trey, and leave it there? Believe He would sort things out for their sake? And what about Trey? Could she trust him to forgive her for everything? "All day today I kept looking over my shoulder, hoping to see him standing there. He never came."

Melissa gave her a hug. "Give Trey time. If he's the man for you, this won't stop him from pursuing a relationship."

"I'm not too sure about that. Who wants a relationship with a broken woman?"

"A man who knows the power of Mighty God, the Great Physician. He's not only the Healer of our physical bodies, but of our hearts, minds, and souls. He wants what's best. Why not put Him back on the throne of your life and heart where He used to be?"

"It's not that easy."

"No, it's not. It's a decision—a choice. He will guide and direct your steps, so you can make good choices. And whoever the Lord has for you to love and to be loved by in return, He will prepare the way for things to work out, regardless of your past."

"I want to, Melissa. I do, but I don't know how."

"Can I pray for you?"

Karianne's heart raced. Not from fear, but from the foreign feeling of hope.

As Karianne lay in bed reading, she listened to Jake's labored breathing coming from the corner of the bedroom. She rolled over and caught sight of his paw jerking in the air. "What are you dreaming about, my sweet boy? Are you thinking about the past like me?"

Having read the same page twice, she set her book on the nightstand and rested against her pillow, her thoughts lost on Jake and how his PTSD brought him home. His life was different now, but the baggage he carried from Iraq meant the vacuum and hair dryer frightened him easily. It was part of who he was, but no matter what he feared, he was still wanted, needed, and loved.

She loved Jake, and as Trey said, he was a gift from the Lord. So, if the Lord cared about Jake and his well-being, how much more would the Lord care about her? She might be broken, but like Jake, she wasn't destroyed, incapable of loving and living again.

Maybe with God's help, she'd be able to find herself again—her new self—one with a past, but also with a glorious future.

CHAPTER 11

$\mathcal{I}$t was hard to leave Jake on the first day of the festival, but Karianne planned to spend the morning cheering on her friends Amabelle and Patrick from inside the hot air balloon gondola.

The race to the Atlantic was huge for Helen, bringing participants from across the country. Even Amabelle and Patrick were thrilled to enter the competition and join with local ballooning enthusiasts.

Turning into the Wilkins launch field, Karianne gazed at the large display of shaped balloons. Each one, different in design and more sharply patterned than the next, matched the colors of the rainbow. On her fifth pass through the lot, she found a parking space.

Amabelle waved as Karianne got out of the car and hurried toward her. "I thought you were going to miss us."

"I couldn't find a place to park, but I don't think it's seven yet." She checked her watch.

"We finished a bit early, and with Patrick's excitement, I was afraid he might leave you behind. Come on."

They soon made it to the launch site, where Patrick and another man waited in the balloon.

Patrick smiled as they approached. "There you are." He helped her and his wife aboard. "Karianne, I want you to meet the captain of our ship, Cole Masterson. He'll be taking us to the Atlantic. Cole, this here is our friend, Karianne."

"Glad you could join us," the older man said, fueling the burner with a short burst of flame. "Have you flown in a balloon before?"

"No, it's my first time. I am a tiny bit nervous."

Amabelle leaned into her shoulder and whispered, "You'll do great. I'm so glad you came."

She squeezed Amabelle's hand. "I am too. Thank you for inviting me."

"The race has begun," Cole said. "Are you ready?"

At the question, her stomach gave way to queasiness. Her life was full of fear, but today she was going to face it head on. This was her first step of many. "Yes, sir. More than you'll ever know."

With the ropes untied, the captain fueled the burner, lifting them off the ground. Unsteadied by the movement, she swayed but then righted herself, catching sight of Trey as she did.

He was here. Had he come to see her?

No. They'd never talked about her participating in this race because she hadn't accepted Amabelle's invitation until this morning. So why was he here, and who was he with? As her mind worked, Trey walked toward another man. Dillon. And why was he back?

"You all right?"

She forced her focus off Trey and noticed how high they'd risen. Her gaze settled on the Chattahoochee River, winding its way across the county below. "Look!" She pointed. "There's the Helendorf Inn. The river. Everything looks different from up here."

"Check out the town," Patrick said, drawing Karianne's attention to the red roofs, which appeared smaller as the balloon rose.

"I love the mountains." Amabelle's wistful tone sent Karianne's focus to the Blue Ridge Mountains. "Aren't they spectacular? By the work of His hands, He gave us this world to enjoy."

Never had Karianne seen such natural beauty as in this moment. The very presence of God felt almost tangible. How had she missed this—missed Him—for so long? It seemed like the Lord Himself was guiding the balloon so she wouldn't miss His glory on display.

Oh, Lord. I'm sorry for walking away. Sorry for putting Ron before you. Sorry for not trusting You with my future. Lord, I give my life back to you. Right here, right now, in this balloon gondola.

Tears filled her eyes, and she chuckled.

Amabelle touched her arm. "Are you crying or laughing?"

Karianne turned to them, tears of joy streaming down her cheeks. She didn't even care if the pilot saw her. She wanted to scream her joy from the mountaintops. "You don't know how much I needed this today. God met me here. In the air. He revealed Himself to me. He's never left me, not even when I walked away from Him. I've had such a hard life, but He wants me anyway. I've given Him everything—my past, my future, my trust—from this moment forward."

"Oh, Karianne." Amabelle hugged her close, then returned to Patrick as Karianne quietly watched the countryside pass below.

Too soon, the balloon shifted slightly. Everyone seemed to hold their breath as the pilot turned on the burner. The hot air balloon began to turn, and a few moments later, descended.

Before long, the pilot maneuvered them around trees to land in an open field. They'd only been in flight thirty minutes before the balloon came down in the middle of nowhere.

But Karianne didn't mind. For the first time in a long time, she was right where she needed to be.

Trey followed Dillon out of the restaurant, and seeing an auburn-haired woman across the street, he searched for Karianne in the crowd. He had heard her balloon landed a couple of hours ago. He wanted to see her—to talk—but should he?

"You haven't said much since you saw Karianne lift off this morning."

Trey turned from the window of one of the Bavarian-styled shops to face Dillon. "I guess I haven't noticed."

"Who are you trying to fool? I know you have feelings for Kari. It was obvious the first time you called and

asked about her. Now, seeing you sulk around town …
This isn't like you."

There was no need to deny it, but what had happened
between him and Karianne … He didn't know where to
go from there. "I admit I have feelings for her, but what
good is it if she doesn't trust me?"

Dillon considered that. "Then the question should be,
how do you gain someone's trust?"

He'd tossed and turned for the last two nights, asking
the same question. "I wish I knew."

"By trusting the Lord and following after Him. Love
Kari when she isn't lovable. Forgive her when she hurts
you. Don't give up on her when she's given up on herself
or you. When she can't pray, pray for her, and with her.
Be there."

Trey slowed his steps. "Unconditional love. Even if
she tries to put me in jail, I should love her anyway.
Forgive her. Pray for her. Never give up on her or us."

"Exactly." A smile spread across Dillon's face. "So you
love Kari? Your words, not mine."

Trey groaned. He'd opened himself up for that one.
"I know it's too soon. We met only a few weeks ago, but in
the time we've spent together, I can see us having a future.
Like God had us cross paths. I mean, I've been praying
for some random woman these last three years. My heart
even stirred for her at different times during prayer. And
now that I've met her, I think He's been preparing me this
entire time."

"I can see it. I felt the same way when you first told
me about coming to Helen."

"But what happens if I'm wrong? About everything. And she isn't the one?"

"I think you know, and by the way you've been pouting all day, I know."

"What? I have not been pouting." Trey stood taller. "I'm a grown man with a successful construction company, and because I'm wildly successful, I branched out with a starter company. Men like me don't pout."

Dillon raised a brow. "Then what do you call it?"

What did he call it? Trey shook his head. "I got nothing."

Dillon laughed. "You, my friend, have one option. When do you plan on seeing Kari?"

"I was thinking I might text and ask if she'd meet me here tonight. They have balloon rides. Maybe take one up together."

"That would be nice. Lauren and I will be going out for dinner. We might run into each other. See how it's going."

"If I'm pouting, don't bother."

"Gotcha. You ready to head back?"

"Yeah. The city council has agreed to give me the key to the facility where the fireworks are being kept. I'll be heading there and checking them out. I'm not sure how they were handled when they were moved. All the connections need to be intact for Saturday night, or we won't be having much of a fireworks show after all. I'm praying everything goes smoothly."

"You'll do great. Lauren and I can't wait to see them." Dillon pointed to a parking lot to the right. "I think we're over there."

"Hey, do you mind driving back? I should text Karianne before it gets too late and she makes other plans."

"Sure."

Trey tossed Dillon the keys as they neared the car. Once he got in, he typed out a message. *Do you have plans tonight around 7 p.m.? If not, I'd like to talk. Can you meet me in front of the Hot & Sweet Coffee and Ice Cream Shop on Chattahoochee Street off Main?*

Delivered popped up under his text. A few seconds later, she was texting back.

I'm sorry, Trey. I've made plans. Can we meet sometime tomorrow?

His heart sank. Tomorrow wouldn't work. Several council members had asked him to join them for lunch, then he'd be preparing the mounting system for the fireworks.

Tomorrow is a big day, and I'm not sure I'll have extra time.

I understand. If you discover you have some free time, let me know. When is your flight?

First thing Sunday morning.

Do you need a ride?

I had planned to take a taxi.

Trey, let me take you.

He could imagine the sound of his name on her lips, and it almost did him in. Was this the last time he'd see Karianne? Was this part of God's plan?

Are you sure?

I'd like to.

Okay, I'll call you after the festival with the details.

Sounds good. Talk to you soon.

He gave a thumbs-up emoji, feeling anything but

okay. He glanced out the car window. They were parked in Dillon's driveway. "We're here."

"Five minutes ago. Everything all right?"

"She's going to drive me to the airport. It'll be the last time we see each other."

Dillon looked at him dubiously. "You're sure? It doesn't have to be."

"Aren't you taking your wife to dinner?"

"All right, all right. Subject dropped. See you inside." Dillon closed the door behind him and jogged inside.

Trey got out of the car and glanced toward the dog park. How he would miss their times together. No matter how short-lived they were, he'd always remember her smile, the way she laughed, the heart of a woman he yearned to love.

CHAPTER 12

*C*rowds walking Main Street blocked Karianne's view as she hunted for a parking spot. Melissa had asked if she wanted to carpool with her and Brian, but Karianne didn't want to be stuck with the family if things didn't go well between her and Harper. Really, she wanted to be with Trey, having coffee and ice cream, sharing the last moments he'd be in town. Who knew if he'd ever come back after everything she put him through?

But tonight wasn't about her and Trey. It was about laying herself bare, sharing truth in love, and asking those she'd wronged for forgiveness. It felt odd to think about her being open and not worrying about the retaliation or fear that would follow. She would no longer be a victim but a free woman, breaking chains that had entrapped her for so long.

Karianne had a future the Lord had prepared in advance for her. She couldn't wait to discover what it was, or who it might be with, regardless of how hard it might be. Her heart was already changing—she could sense it within her—but she had hurdles to overcome and a past she needed help dealing with. Thankfully, Melissa knew a woman from the hospital who counseled others in abusive relationships. While Ron wasn't with her anymore, the lasting effects of their life together were engraved in her thoughts, hurts, and reactions, and she needed to deal with and heal from them. She could do that now, because God would be with her every step of the way.

Karianne finally found a place to park and hurried to the restaurant, where Melissa's family should have arrived five minutes ago. Music met her as she entered, and just within the doors stood clusters of people waiting to be seated.

"Hi, what's the last name?" the young hostess asked, grabbing a menu.

"I'm meeting a party. The name is Dixon."

"Yes, they were just seated. Follow me."

Karianne tucked her clutch under her arm and rounded the corner as Melissa and Harper came toward her. "I see my friends. Thank you."

"Enjoy your meal." The hostess left.

Melissa was first to reach her.

"I'm sorry I'm late."

Melissa waved her off. "Nonsense. You're right on time."

"I'm glad you're here." Harper placed an arm around her shoulders, just as he'd done in the coffee shop, and kissed her temple.

She froze, looking to Melissa for help, but what kind of help could she give? It wasn't up to her friend to set things straight between the two of them. She stepped away from his arms. "Melissa, I need a few minutes with Harper. Do you mind?"

"Of course not." She glanced toward the table. "The waiter is still taking our orders. What would you like?"

Karianne ran down the menu in her mind, then decided on her usual. "Salmon with rice pilaf and green beans."

"Will do." Melissa gave her a reassuring touch on the arm before leaving them.

She glanced at Harper. "Did you need to place your order?"

"They already took it. Would you like to talk outside? It would be quieter."

"Yes, thank you."

Harper placed his hand on her back, directing her outside. Once in the parking lot, they started toward Main Street. "So what did you want to talk about? It seems somewhat important with the way Melissa seemed to be reassuring you."

"It is." Karianne's voice broke. Feeling a little over-whelmed, she cleared her throat. "It's about us."

They paused before crossing Main Street to Munich Strasse, the same street as the wedding chapel. She stopped them in front of Old Thyme Portraits. "Harper, Melissa mentioned you were planning something for us, so I knew we needed to talk. There's something I need to tell you, confess really." Her knees began to quiver.

He nodded toward a bench near the entrance of the store. "Want to sit?"

Could he see her shaking? "That would be great."

She sat and shifted in his direction, swallowing hard. "Harper, I need to apologize to you, and there's no easy way to say this, so I'm just going to come right out with it. I lied to you." She waited for a reaction, but nothing came, so she pressed on. "Trey and I, we weren't dating. Never were."

"I had a feeling."

He knew? "How?"

"Well, Melissa has talked you up for over a year to me, how we'd be perfect for each other. She even got Brian involved, so when you mentioned having a boyfriend, it didn't fit. Plus, Melissa never mentioned anything about another guy."

"No, she wouldn't, because there wasn't anyone. She never mentioned you liked wine now and again either."

"She wouldn't have, since I never shared it. Brian had told me a little about your late fiancé, and after our time together last year, I didn't want you to be turned off. I thought if we went together to a tasting, you could see this working between us, regardless of the past. I think it backfired. I pushed too hard on our first date."

That was for sure. "You were pretty adamant about going, and that made me nervous."

"So who came up with the plan for you and Trey to be in a relationship to scare me off?"

"It was my idea."

"Lucky guy. I would have jumped at the idea too."

"Really? But it didn't seem to affect you at all. You seemed more determined. So much so, you seemed almost like a different person than the one I met last year."

94

"Because I am." He glanced away, toward the restaurant, and sighed softly. "Last year when I came, I had just ended a two-year relationship. It was rocky to say the least. I never meant to find someone I could be remotely interested in, but to get my family off my back, I thought I could at least meet you. You were such a surprise. I was taken aback at how beautiful and kindhearted you were, yet so insecure. You drew me. You weren't like any other woman I'd dated, but because I wasn't ready to date anyone at the time, I didn't push."

"The real reason you never called."

"Yeah. When I returned home, my ex wanted to try again. We finally ended it a few months later."

"I'm sorry."

"I needed time to figure things out, be on my own for a while, so I went to Italy. While I was there, my friend Arlene mentioned she and I should go out sometime, but you were the one I thought of. I really wanted us to work out."

"I did too … but I'm afraid my heart has taken another path."

"Trey?"

"Yeah, but I didn't handle things very well. I messed things up between us. I'm not sure where we stand, or whether we could even be called friends now."

"If what I saw between you and Trey at the coffee shop was any indication of his feelings for you, you have nothing to worry about. He doesn't seem like a man who'd be driven away easily."

Then why hadn't he tried to reach out before today?

"I wish that were true."

He covered her hand with his. "Karianne, if you really care about Trey as you say you do, you need to tell him how you feel."

If only it were that simple. "I want to, but I don't know where to begin."

"Bring him to this bench and lay it all out."

She lowered her voice. "I'm sorry things didn't work out."

Harper stared into the distance. "Me too."

"Maybe we'll both find what we're looking for."

Harper's gaze found hers. "Maybe." He held on to her hand and brought them both to their feet. "Ready to eat?"

"Sounds good to me."

Harper drew her close and kissed her temple again. "Talk to Trey."

She pulled back to look at him. "As long as you ask Arlene out."

He smiled, his eyes brightening. "Deal."

With Dillon and Lauren out for dinner, Trey wasn't in the mood to eat alone. He'd rather be in a crowd and get lost in the noise. He'd heard of a great steak place with live music, so he drove to Paul's Steakhouse off Main Street. Afterward, he could catch a balloon ride, although it wouldn't be the same without Karianne.

Nothing seemed to be the same without Karianne, and to know he wouldn't see her until the drive to the airport made him anxious. There was little he could do with her having obligations tonight. With his lunch with the city council tomorrow, he'd have to wait to tell her how he felt. He wasn't sure she'd be receptive, but he had to try.

Trey pulled up to the restaurant and took the last remaining parking spot facing Main Street. Turning off the car, he glanced up to see Karianne and Harper standing near a bench across the street.

He'd forgotten. Their family dinner. *She decided to go.*

His stomach bottomed, and his pulse raced. Maybe it was the night, the atmosphere of the festival, the people walking around, but they seemed lost in their own world, the two of them alone. As Harper leaned in and kissed Karianne at her temple, he seemed to whisper something. Karianne pulled back, but then they both smiled and turned in Trey's direction.

Should he hide? Drive away? He couldn't face her right now. Maybe it was better not to face her at all. Maybe he should call a taxi tomorrow as he'd planned.

Harper and Karianne continued his way but veered as they neared the restaurant. Thankfully, he was parked by the street and not the entrance.

As Trey left the parking lot, he glanced in the rearview mirror and caught sight of Harper's hand on her back as they entered the restaurant.

He lost his appetite.

CHAPTER 13

On Saturday, the last day of the festival, Karianne hadn't been able to find Trey anywhere. She'd stopped by Dillon's earlier, but he said Trey had left for a meeting that would last until late that afternoon. Now, she scanned the horizon dotted with hot air balloons and took in the view one last time before the sun set.

Deciding to take matters into her own hands, she searched Trey out, finally finding him and a few others in a secluded area off the Chattahoochee as they prepared for the show. Should she say something now or wait until the fireworks ended?

Karianne looked to her watch. Fifteen minutes before the show started, darkness began to settle in. Not wanting to ruin things for him again, she stayed behind the fenced-in area.

Several people talked nearby, but she couldn't distinguish the voices or what they were saying. Fully aware of how much rode on this fireworks show, she closed her eyes in prayer. *Lord, please be with Trey and whoever is helping him. Let everything go smoothly. Amen.*

Whatever the Lord held in store for Trey and her was a mystery. All she knew was she wanted to share everything with him, especially what had been said between her and Harper, and she needed to apologize for involving him in her deception. Trey had only been trying to help, but he ended up on the wrong side of the bargain once she landed him at the police station. They still hadn't talked about what happened, although Trey had asked her out for dinner last night. She hoped that was a good sign, that he still wanted to spend time with her after everything. Telling Trey no had been difficult, but she was glad she and Harper had a chance to talk.

A loud hiss cut through the quiet, followed by two more, and Karianne sought the night sky. A large firework boomed gold, followed by two others in red and green. Her breath hitched at the size of the explosion and how close they seemed. More fireworks sailed into the air with expert precision, one after another, some with shapes, including hot air balloons, some with glittery aftereffects, some with a spreading effect that reminded her of the old sprinkler she had in the yard when she was a child. The sheer beauty mesmerized her, and to think Trey was the one to orchestrate it all.

As the grand finale exploded into the night sky, leaving behind a whitish grey cloud, she stood in awe of the man behind what she had just witnessed. A man who took a step of faith and followed his dreams. Strolling to the gate of the safety barrier, she called out, "Trey Scott. Can I speak to Trey Scott, please?"

The gate opened, and an older man smiled at her. "Can I help you, miss?"

"Um, I'd like to speak to Trey Scott, please."

"Is he expecting you?"

"No, sir, but I'd still like to see him."

"Let me check if he's available."

Karianne nodded. "Thank you." A minute later, her phone chimed.

I'm in the middle of clean up. We can talk at the dog park. How's ten?

Was he too busy to see her? Tell her in person? She looked at the time on her cell. An hour till then. *I'll bring Jake. See you then.*

She waited for a reply, but none came.

Trey leashed Whiskers and took a deep breath. He had mixed feelings about meeting Karianne, but he couldn't keep her waiting. He'd never liked her going to the park at night, but when she wanted to see him after the fireworks, he didn't have another option. He didn't want others to hear their conversation.

He led Whiskers across the street to where Karianne sat in a circumference of white light, a lamp at her feet. Jake barked in the distance. "Nice lamp."

"Hey," she said, the pitch in her voice signaling her surprise. She rose quickly and met him a foot from the bench. "Trey, the fireworks were wonderful. You did such an amazing job. Have you heard back from the city? Surely you'll get the account."

He looked away, saddened he wouldn't be returning. He'd hire someone to travel in his place. "I got the account for the next three years."

"Congratulations ... I think." Her expression sobered. "What's the matter?"

He didn't answer.

"I know I hurt you, Trey, by asking you to pretend to be dating me, by calling the police. I can only guess that you're sorry for meeting me. If I could take it back, I would."

What? No. "Who said anything about having regrets about meeting you? Karianne, I'm not sorry we met. And I'm especially not sorry you asked me to help you. Do I wish we could redo the whole police and FBI interrogation? Of course. It confused and hurt me, but I forgave you."

"You forgave me without my asking?"

The astonishment in her tone drew his gaze. Never had he felt such clear purpose as he did at this moment. God was calling him to love Karianne, to always forgive, to be patient, and to point her to Him. "I'll always forgive you. A hundred times over."

"Thank you," she whispered, blinking her watery eyes.

Trey tied Whiskers to the fence and took Karianne's hand, bringing her to the bench with him. "I need to tell you something," he said as they sat down.

Whatever news she thought he'd share, apprehension scrolled across her face and tightened her fingers around his. "Sounds serious."

"You know how close Dillon and I are?"

"Yes."

"About six years ago, Dillon called and asked if I'd pray for someone. He never told me any details, only that a friend of his needed prayer. At first, he didn't mention a name, but about three years ago, he called her Kari, and told me her fiancé died while driving under the influence."

She frowned. "Dillon. He asked you to pray for me?"

"He did, but I had no idea who you were. Then when I came to town and saw you at the dog park, it was like something inside me clicked. I had to meet you. It wasn't until our second day at the park that I put the pieces together and realized you were the woman Dillon had asked me to pray for. I was blown away and called him about it."

"You knew everything?" She slipped her hand from his. "Even when I came to your house and poured my heart out about my life with Ron?"

He lowered his voice in admission. "I didn't know everything."

"But you knew?"

Her chin dipped, and he squeezed her hand. "Some things. Dillon never mentioned Ron outside of conversations about college until his passing. I know this is going to sound strange, but I think the Lord was preparing my heart for when we met. I believe that's why this—us—is so easy. It's the reason that, regardless of your past, I will always be here for you."

"I know you're probably thinking I'm this weak woman, and as Harper said—"

"Karianne, you're anything but weak. You're just

trying to heal from hurts so deep that you're not sure who to trust. What would've happened if I'd told you right off that I knew about Ron? How would you have responded?"

She thought for a moment, meeting his gaze. "I don't know."

"I do. You would've pushed me away and never given me a chance. Yet, here we are. You're reaching out, needing me in your life, and I'm wearing my heart on my sleeve, needing you in mine. I fell in love with you at first sight, Karianne. God knew, so He led me to pray for you before we ever met." He swallowed. "Can I admit something else?"

She hesitated, then nodded.

"Last night I was at Paul's Steakhouse, and I saw you with Harper. He kissed you."

Her cheeks tinted pink, and she tucked a strand of hair behind her ear. "I was with Harper last night, but it wasn't what you think. I told him the truth about our dating but admitted to having feelings for you. We were saying good-bye."

He closed his eyes, relief washing over him. "I was afraid that—"

"Trey Scott, from the moment I met you, I haven't been able to stop thinking of you." She pressed her hand against his chest. "You have such a big heart, a gentle spirit, a handsome smile ... eyes that at times I feel lost in. I'm not ready for a serious relationship—God has work to do in my life first—but I can picture you in my future. Really, I don't think I want to imagine my future without you."

He covered her hand over his heart. "Does that mean you don't mind dating a guy who sets off fireworks for a living?"

She smiled. "I'd be honored."

"May I kiss you, Karianne?"

Her grin brightened. "I'd like that."

He gently cupped her cheek and pressed a kiss against her lips. There were no words, but none were needed. It was a promise of a future yet to come.

EPILOGUE

ime flashed before Trey's eyes and vanished like the wind. During the past year, Trey had flown back to Helen every month and stayed for a weekend to officially date Karianne. Thankfully, his time away had been good for them both.

Karianne started going to counseling. At first, she was concerned what others would say if they found out. Trey tried to nurture the idea of seeking help from a counselor by sharing scriptures where the Lord wanted her to be free of fear and to forgive herself and Ron. God was opening new doors and a new life for both of them. Trey could hardly wait.

Over those months she had called him, sometimes cheerfully, sometimes upset and sometimes even wanting to throw things. During those times, God worked on her physical, mental, and spiritual healing. She spoke of God more, allowed Trey into her deepest thoughts, genuinely laughed more, and started wishing him closer.

Even though he and Karianne never spoke of

marriage, he started sensing it was time. He purchased several acres outside of town, and over the months, built a two-story, four-bedroom home. When he was in Ohio, he spent time settling the business end of things with his brother so he could help run the company from Helen. Trey even hired a manager to run everyday operations at the fireworks store in Ohio.

Today, nearly one year after their kiss at the dog park, was the first day of the hot air balloon race to the Atlantic, and Karianne thought he wasn't coming into town until tomorrow. Little did she know Trey had enlisted Melissa and her friends Amabelle and Patrick for a surprise he hoped and prayed Karianne would accept.

Karianne had been antsy for the last few days, waiting for Trey to come back to Helen. The months seemed to drag, and with him so far away, she hated to see him leave. When he returned this time, she planned to ask him to stay. Whether he would was another matter altogether. He had many responsibilities in Ohio, and she had just started thinking about moving there when he surprised her by purchasing property to build a house. If only he'd use it. If only…

A year ago, she hadn't been sure how she felt about marriage and intimacy, but her life had changed inside and out, and now she was ready. Trey had been so patient and understanding. God had revealed to her what it was like to truly be loved. It wasn't about the heat of a kiss or physical attraction, though she now looked forward to being married to Trey. It was about a spiritual attraction. To the man who prayed for her long before they met. To the man who gave her space for the Lord to work and heal the past. To the man who wanted what God wanted above all else. Trey Scott was the love of her life, and she thanked the Lord for him every day.

Melissa huffed. "Karianne, you need to hurry, or we'll miss seeing Patrick and Amabelle before liftoff."

Amabelle had mentioned taking pictures for some news article before liftoff, but Karianne's makeup had taken longer than normal, especially when her thoughts roamed to Trey.

"I can't wait until he comes home."

"I know, but that's tomorrow. Let's think about today."

"Party pooper." Karianne gave her friend a wink, then stared at her white quarter-sleeve shirt and peach-and black-striped scarf. "Is the scarf all right for photos?"

"You look great. It goes great with the jeans. Now can we leave?"

Karianne chuckled, nabbed her purse from the couch, and scratched Jake behind the ears before locking up her apartment.

Ten minutes later, Melissa pulled into the Wilkins launch field and parked. "I hope we're not late." She slipped from the driver's seat and waited for Karianne before locking the doors.

Karianne looked to her watch. "It's not launch time yet." She glanced around, finding Patrick and Cole's hot air balloon. "It's over there." She pointed to the multicol-ored teardrop-shaped balloon. "See, they're still there."

Melissa hurried along, dragging Karianne with her.

As they neared the balloon, Karianne noticed another crew member with them. "Amabelle didn't tell me they had hired another ..." The man had his back to her, but she'd recognize those broad shoulders anywhere. "Trey!"

He swung around and gave her the smile she had dreamt about only last night.

Karianne ran. She needed to touch him to be sure he was truly here.

Trey opened his arms and caught her against him. "Did you miss me?"

"I can't believe you're here." She squeezed him closer, taking in the feel of him and the smell of his clean-scented aftershave.

"I've missed you too," he whispered into her hair. "I couldn't wait another day."

Lately, it seemed like a part of her was missing until they were together. He completed her and gave her a glimpse of Scripture, where the two would become one. "I've missed you."

"We need to shove off if you plan to join the race," Patrick said from the gondola.

Trey climbed in.

She glanced at the others. "Patrick, there's not enough room for all of us. What about Cole and Amabelle?"

Amabelle snickered. "Karianne, don't worry. I'd already planned to sit this one out. My wise husband mentioned Cole and I needed to check out the competition. Melissa volunteered to go with us. You better hurry before Patrick leaves you behind. Have fun. We'll see ya at the Atlantic." She turned and waved over her shoulder.

Karianne took hold of Trey's strong hand, and he helped her into the gondola. It was more than a wicker basket to her. It represented the moment he first prayed for her. She'd been nameless—a total stranger—yet God entrusted her to his care. And here she was now, without physical unity, entrusting Trey with her life, heart, mind, and body.

"You ready?" He stepped to her side, shifting the weight evenly for launch. After collecting her hand, he brought it to his cheek. His eyes closed as if in prayer, but before she could ask, his eyes opened.

Patrick cast off the ropes and fueled the burner, lifting them into the air.

"Wow." Trey looked out at the city of Helen—the shops and restaurants—and wrapped an arm around her waist. "Beyond the trees. Check out those mountains. God's masterpiece."

She leaned against him, in awe of the moment. "So beautiful."

"Karianne?"

"Hmm?"

"If you could have anything in this world, what would it be?"

She slid from his embrace and faced him. He looked so serious that she almost questioned him. Instead, she needed him to know her answer, the truth she'd finally share. "Without a doubt, to marry you. Tomorrow if I could."

His face lightened, and a smile set her at ease. "Tomorrow?"

"You asked."

"Can I ask you another question?"

She grinned at the mischievous glint in his eyes. "Of course."

From his pocket, he withdrew a small black box and lowered to one knee. She covered her mouth with her hand as tears filled her eyes.

"Karianne, will you marry me?"

"Tomorrow?" she breathed.

He chuckled. "Well, as soon as my family can join us."

"Yes, Trey Scott!"

He rose to his feet, and Karianne wrapped her arms around his neck. She still couldn't comprehend what God had done in her life, but she knew it was called grace. At first it had fallen softly with her tears. Now, a year later, she walked in that same grace, breathed it in as lifegiving air. That same grace had brought her here, to the arms of a man who truly loved her and she loved in return.

Soon they'd be entrusting their marriage to the One who'd made their hearts one.

CONTEMPORARY ROMANCE

To Gain a Mommy

GAINING LOVE NOVELLA BOOK ONE

Thirteen years ago, pediatrician Hope Michaels was the fool-hearted girl who came home from college to learn the man she loved was engaged to her twin. But now to move on with her life and accept a proposal of marriage, she must confront the one man who holds the key to the wounds of her past. Fire Captain Carl McGuire can put out any flame, except for the one Hope sparks within him. As she stirs up his life and heart, Carl knows some things never change. Even a past he'd rather keep hidden. When a new neighbor moves in across the street who would be a perfect fit for their family, Mary and Brody form a plan to bring their dad and Hope together. But how will it work if Hope keeps pushing him away?

GAINING LOVE NOVELLA BOOK TWO

Pediatrician Patrick Reynolds works wonders with sick children, yet when it comes to pets, he's clueless. But caring for his sister's menagerie while she's on vacation is the perfect answer to working through a broken engagement. Hoping to escape the memories, he returns to his hometown, the last place he'd expect to find love. Life as a single mom is never easy, but pet shop owner Amabelle Durand has found contentment. When an old friend returns to care for his sister's pets, he enlists her assistance to keep the animals alive. But when Amabelle's young daughter falls ill, she finds herself attracted to more than the handsome pediatrician's medical skills. As Valentine's Day approaches, will Patrick and Amabelle miss out on the love they've always desired? Or will their love take flight under the stars on this very special night?

To Gain a Bodyguard

Gaining Love Novella Book Three

Undercover agent Madi Reynolds has spent years infiltrating a human-trafficking ring, but when her life is threatened, she is advised to leave the country with her bodyguard. War Veteran and ICE agent Brice Johnson has been defending his country and American lives for as long as he can remember. Now, he faces the biggest assignment of his life—protect the woman he loves. He's never been one to run from a fight, but when crippling visions of war call out to him, he begins to wonder if surrender is an option after all.

Gaining Love Novella Book Four

Karianne Bennett, small-town wedding coordinator, has always believed in happily-ever-afters. That is, for everyone but herself. But then hope comes when she adopts a retired service dog and a cat-walking newcomer catches her eye. Trey Scott has been fascinated with fireworks since he was a boy. If he can land the festival account in an out-of-state town, he'll be that much closer to achieving his lifelong goal. His dreams never included a beautiful dog walker who also happens to be the stranger he's been praying over for years.

Unending Love Series Book One

Elizabeth Roberts can't remember her past, and the present is too painful. She turns to nightclubs and drinking to forget her infant daughter's death, her husband's affair. When his wife's coma wiped out the memory of their marriage, Chris Roberts found comfort elsewhere. He can't erase his betrayal, but with God's help he's determined to fight for Elizabeth at any cost. She wants to forget. He wants to save his marriage. Can they trust God with their future and find a love that's unconditional?

Restored

UNENDING LOVE SERIES BOOK TWO

Dr. Steven Moore is known nationally for saving lives. If only he could save his own. Unable to deal with his prognosis, he retreats to a happier time in his past—to the woman who once stole his heart. Four years after the death of her beloved husband, bookstore owner Elizabeth Roberts still struggles to sustain her faith and joy in the Lord as she raises her two sons.

She strives to find a way through her family's grief, never suspecting a man from her past might offer hope for her future. But how can there be a future when he's only come to kiss her and says good-bye?

The Rescue

ALL ROADS LEAD TO TEXAS SERIES BOOK ONE

Rosalind Standford's life shatters when she is forced into a betrothal to a cunning banker. But when a telegram arrives announcing the man who captured her heart is on a train to Boston, Rosalind must hide her true feelings before the thin cord of her existence unravels the deadly secrets she keeps. Cowboy Trent Easton returns to his roots in Boston society to find his childhood friend, now a broken woman, engaged to a man close to her father's age. Though she once rejected him, when Trent learns she's in danger, he determines to do whatever it takes to keep her safe—even taking her to the altar in the black of night. But will his name and the remote wilds of his Texas ranch be enough to protect her? Or will freedom cost them their lives?

All Roads Lead to Texas Series Book Two

Coming Winter 2020

Jessica Thomson is fleeing the man who killed her father. But her stagecoach is robbed, and when the stranger who rescues her declares she will be his wife, she does the only thing she knows to do—shove her revolver in his back. Never would she have expected he wore a star on his chest. Too bad she vowed never to love another lawman. As sheriff, Blake McKenny prides himself on protecting his town's people from danger, but his efforts didn't include a headstrong woman bent on putting herself in harm's way. When outlaws threaten his town and put Jessica's life in danger, Blake's failure to save his late wife haunts him. Can Jessica and Blake forgive themselves for the past and protect each other—even if that costs them their hearts in the process?

MORE ABOUT TANYA EAVENSON

Tanya Eavenson is an award-winning Christian romance novelist. She enjoys spending time with her husband and their three children. Her favorite pastime is grabbing a cup of coffee, eating chocolate, and reading a good book. You can find her at her website, Facebook, or at her readers group, Tanya's Books & More.